GHOSTS *of* PLUM RUN

Vol. 1 - Beginnings

Timothy Russo

DEDICATION

To my great grandparents, who were immigrants

CONTENTS

ACKNOWLEDGMENTS

Many thanks to Tim Orr, Darryl Sannes, Wayne Jorgenson, Deb McCauslin, Dean Schultz, John Heiser, Matt Atkinson, Chris Osgood, Jim DeMay, Brian Leehan, the Codori family, Tom Schroeder, all the people at the Gettysburg National Military Park, the Minnesota Historical Society, and the Cuyahoga County Public Library. Special thanks to my Patreon subscribers, whose patronage online made this book possible. The most thanks go to my mother.
Thanks Mom, I love you.

1 MAG DEVIT

Mag knew the moon was white

Little Margaret Devit first became a rebel over the colors of the rainbow. One July 4th, about 1839, age 3, Mag's mother took her to Gettysburg's modest fireworks celebration, where Mama taught Mag about colors using the American flag. "Red, white, and blue", Mama said to Little Mag, pointing up and down all the flags lining the town's streets. A full moon brightened the summer night.

"White, like the moon?" Mag asked Mama.

"Yes, Mag. The moon is white, just like those stars and stripes."

Black is the color that confused the toddler most, as she shot up tall faster than just about all the kids around. Black was confusing because everyone told Mag she was black, but plainly, Mag was not black. The night sky is black. Coal for the stove, that's black. Mag's skin? That ain't black. Mag's mama didn't talk about her papa much, except to say that his white innards mixed with hers to make Mag "less black".

"That's what white men do with black women," Mama sneered, "- leave their innards in 'em, then run off". Mag never knew her father. Mama would never speak of him. Gettysburg's African American population had many such mixed families, torn apart as soon as they came together. This color should not mix with that one. Single mothers thus proliferated, left to explain the unexplainable to children who didn't look much like their mothers.

"Why ain't I grey then?" Mag asked. "If your innards are black, and my papa's were white, shouldn't I be grey?"

It was the first time Mag's mama slapped her. Hard.

Mag knew those "white" people in town weren't "white", either. All you had to do was look at 'em, especially when they bent over, their pants slipped down, and their hind quarters blazed out at her, crack and all. "That ain't white," she'd say to Mama, walking down Long Lane to their little shack on Abraham Brien's farm, just south of Gettysburg.

"You want another slap?" Mama snapped.

"You said the moon is white, like the stars and stripes, and that ain't white," Mag insisted. "Mr. Brien ain't even black, either!" Mag pushed, holding Mama's hand as they hurried home from doing the "white folk's" laundry. "He might be really brown, but he ain't..."

Mag got slapped again.

One day, Mama sent Little Mag to the "white" folks' house with laundry to deliver. When the door opened, the lady of the house was horrified.

"Those linens are not WHITE. You take them to your mama and bring them back when they're clean!" Mag looked at the carefully folded bed sheets.

"Ma'am, they sho nuff whiter than you!" Mag got slapped again. Mama told Mag something must have snuck into the washing to stain the sheets, like Papa's innards got into Mama. The last straw came one summer, playing in the fields on Cemetery Ridge near Brien's farm, when a little "black" boy (who was less brown than Mag) told Mag her color was "yellow", like his. They collecting flowers, for church, yellow field flowers.

"Lotta yella folk in these parts," the boy said, holding a dandelion. Then he pointed northward, toward a distant hill, miles away. "Papa say bunch of 'em live up Yella Hill, way over there!" That was it. Soon, Mag stopped listening to anyone. Everyone was lying to her about the colors of the rainbow. If you'll lie about rainbows, you'll lie about anything. Mag looked at the runt of a boy, nearly half her size, making a decision that would change her life.

"I know the moon is white," Mag said to the boy. "And you ain't yella."

Mag sets off to the Quakers

Having decided she wasn't black, or yellow, or anything else but Mag, by age 14 in 1850, little Mag Devit wasn't so little anymore. Towering over every kid her age, Mag was beautiful and strong, inside and out, which is why her mother sent Mag north one very dark rainy night to visit William and Phebe Wright.

"You'll be goin' up the Carlisle Road tomorrow night," Mama told Mag as they got ready for bed in their shack on Abraham Brien's farm. Mag knew this day would come, knew what that trip meant. Staring across the pillow at the back of Mama's head, Mag took a deep breath, then whispered across the pillow.

"How do you know we'll have slaves to run tomorrow?" Mag asked. Mama snapped her head to look at Mag across the pillow. Mother and daughter instantly transformed into comrades in arms. Mag grinned, knowing Mama needed comfort in that moment. Mama sighed.

"Oh Mag," she said, holding back tears. Mama tucked Mag in next to her. "Never could get anything by you."

"I'll get those folks wherever they need to go," Mag answered. Mama turned back on her pillow.

"Now you just get a good night's sleep, tomorrow you'll be happy you did."

The next day, Mag did her chores with extra vim and vigor, excited for her adventure that night. Mama was right; slaves on the run turned up at Mr. Brien's house, announced by Mr. Brien with a knock on the shack door about midnight. Mama let him in out the pouring rain as Mag got dressed in a flash.

"Two boys need runnin' up to Wright's house," Mr. Brien told Mama.

"Abe, it's Mag's turn tonight." Mr. Brien smiled, turning to Mag, who stood at attention, bag over her shoulder, riding hat on, ready to go.

"They're in my wagon under some straw you're deliverin' to Wright's farm," Mr. Brien told Mag, with military precision. "You ready for this?" A pause was filled with the rumble of pounding rain on the roof.

"Mr. Brien, you know I run a good team of

horses, they'll be there in no time at all," Mag declared.

"This rain'll help," Mr. Brien added, trying to comfort the rookie. Mag realized why Mama chose tonight for her debut.

"How'd you know it was gonna rain tonight, Mama?" Mama smiled, taking Mag by her shoulders.

"Slave catchers sho hate gettin' wet!" Everyone laughed, and the tension was gone. The ensuing briefing Mag soaked in from Mama and Mr. Brien for twenty minutes never seemed to end; Don't go too fast, or too slow, watch out for this, pay attention to that, if this, then that...Mag nodded along, eager to get on the road. Finally, Mag was off, driving Mr. Brien's horses the best she could on the muddy road.

Terror gripped Mag for the first time in her life as the team left town. Eight miles never seemed so long. Every turn in the road seized her attention. Mag snapped the reins obsessively, their rhythm and the rain calming her somehow. Half way through, Mag began to enjoy the entire affair, looking back at the soaked straw over her silent passengers. Suddenly, a man waved a lantern on a stretch of the road, directing Mag's wagon to turn right. On the turn, William Wright jumped aboard, patting Mag on the back as she drove the team toward a house, whispering to her.

"Welcome to the Friends' Meeting House!" The

horses splashed through the mud up to Wright's barn, skidding the wagon to a stop. "Let's warm all of you up," Wright declared, walking to the back of the wagon to lift the straw off the slaves underneath. Peering out from under the straw still afraid and soaked to their bones, the slaves needed encouragement, which Mag provided.

"Get on outta there!" Mag whispered loudly, waving her hands. The slaves crawled out of the straw, now more scared of Mag than whoever else might be out there.

"The children are all asleep, just be mindful, the stove is in the corner," Wright whispered as he guided the party into the modest one floor house, a candle glowing from the window of the loft. "I'm sorry to say I haven't met you yet," Wright said to Mag.

"Mag Devit, my mama sent me tonight from Brien's," Mag replied, taking off her wet overcoat and riding hat. Wright noticed how young Mag was, as the slaves tentatively tip toed to the stove through a house filled with sleeping kids. The conversation carried on in hushed tones, William Wright quite accustomed to speaking just quiet enough to keep his children sleeping, yet still be heard. The kids were accustomed to sleeping through it.

"Your mother is a fine lady. Is this your first night on the trail?"

"I suppose that's pretty plain, ain't it," Mag chuckled.

"Please, do sit down for a spell, Miss Devit, but your journey tonight is not yet over I'm afraid." Such politeness from a white man disarmed Mag. The inside of the Quaker home felt other worldly, so peaceful and serene the news she had to keep going was most disappointing. Wright's wife Phebe emerged down from the loft, crossing the room full of sleeping children to pull up chairs to sit around the warmth of the wood stove.

"William, the loft is nearly full," Phebe announced sadly.

"Didn't look like there was room here," Mag noticed.

"I was just telling our guests, thank you, Phebe." The slaves became scared again, forgetting the warm stove momentarily. Wright calmed them quickly. "No, no, we can accommodate you two fine gentlemen in the loft, but I'm afraid you must stay at Mr. Mathews' farm, Miss Devit." Mag had never heard slaves referred to as "fine gentlemen". This Quaker was one strange white man, Mag thought.

"Mathews on Yella Hill?" It was now Mag who disarmed Wright, who smiled, finally relaxing, as Phebe poured hot milk for Mag and the slaves.

"I see your mother taught you well about these

doings, Miss Devit," Wright acknowledged. "I told him you'd be coming, someone anyway, so he may be a bit stand offish when you arrive." Phebe helped the two slaves out of their wet clothes, into dry blankets to sit on the floor near the stove.

"You'll sleep in these blankets," Phebe said, calming their nerves with every breath, seeming angelic. "There are two others like you upstairs, but that just means it'll be warmer tonight. Mr. Mathews has a loft just for you, Miss Devit."

"Normally, we have a bit more room, but tonight the rain has kept us rather more hospitable than usual," Wright explained. After some time warming at the stove, Wright walked Mag back to the wagon. "Miss Devit, I will tell your mother she has nothing to worry about with you on this trail."

"Thank you kindly, Mr. Wright," and she was off again. Wright directed Mag down the road to Edward Mathews at nearby Yellow Hill. For that mile or two, Mag was alone in Mr. Brien's wagon. The rain had subsided, the road unfamiliar, the deep quiet unsettling, so the little cabin with a candle in the window on the crest of Yellow Hill filled Mag with relief.

Inside the crowded cabin, Mathews' sleeping family heard the carriage approach and Papa rustle to greet it. Edward's wife Ann tried to keep the kids in their beds, but it was no use. The six Mathews kids rushed to the windows and doors, the littlest Mathews, Edward Jr. at a year and a half, waddling across the cabin in his diaper following the two oldest to the door; Samuel at 11, Nelson at 9. Nancy, 6, and Jane, 4, stood on the bed peering out the window. William, 2, struggled to get between his two sisters at the window. Mother Ann had trained them all to stay quiet on nights like these, when strangers appeared out of the night.

Ann knew the drill. Up into the loft she crawled, to prepare it for a guest. In the hushed chaos, Edward calmly dressed, exiting past Samuel and Nelson, who watched from the doorway as Edward approached the carriage. Mag stepped down as Edward approached, hands in his pockets, sloshing through the puddles of rain. Mag, drenched, let out a heaving sigh.

"Good evening, ma'am," Edward welcomed with a neighborly hospitality masking deep suspicion. "What brings you to Yellow Hill on this rainy night?" Behind his warm welcome, Edward inspected Mag up and down with steely focus, immediately noticing that like him, Mag, too, was "yellow"; mulatto. Edward's guard came down.

Mag wasn't as professionally clandestine as Edward, yet, but getting there. "I sure hope you got a dry spot for the night, mister! Mag Devit, William Wright sent me here."

The magic words "William Wright" transformed Edward from guarded sentry into practically family.

"Come on in, Miss Devit, let's warm you up."

Pandemonium erupted in the cabin as all the kids saw Papa put his arm around Mag to walk her inside, signaling the all clear. Ann hollered from the loft, "Keep it down!" but again, no use. When the kids saw Mag enter the cabin, looking every bit as "yellow" as they were, well, that was it. There would be no sleep tonight on Yellow Hill. Anne trundled down the ladder from the loft, exasperated that her kids were in a midnight frenzy of welcome.

"Mama, meet Mag," Edward announced. Ann looked her up and down.

"Let's get you out of those clothes," Ann declared. The kids swarmed Mag on cue, disrobed her, wrapped her in a dry blanket, then surrounded Mag all night beside the hearth, an ancient story telling session gripping the cabin until the first birds before dawn sang them all finally to sleep.

Mag learns her superpowers

After her rain soaked midnight journey to Yellow Hill, didn't take long for Mag to realize why Mama kept the slave runnin' to herself while Mag grew up. Instantly, Mag's life doubled, split in two, between daytime in

Gettysburg, and nighttime in the shadows. Simultaneously thrilling and terrifying, Mag came to life, no longer a child, but a young woman with a mission. By day, Mag cleaned and laundered and carried bags for her various white employers. By night, Mag ran slaves. Never the two lives could meet. Not ever.

Soon, Mag became expert in the honeycomb of slave routes outside of town and safe houses in town. For Mag and her mother, it was safest to work on the trail outside of Gettysburg. In town, they were recognizable, spending their days delivering fresh laundry and cleaned rugs, or ferrying passengers' bags from the stagecoach and train station. One slip, and they might give away not just a safe house in town but everything connected to it. An unfriendly laundry customer might be visiting, oh, say, Dobbin's house, see Mag, put two and two together, then all hell would break loose. Mama introduced Mag to the routine with a midnight trip to William Wright's farm for a reason. Those dark roads and isolated farms would remain Mag's beat. Stay on the roads, Mama kept saying.

Problem was, if you were on the roads at night, especially in town, you were necessarily under a cloud of suspicion and a sitting duck for nighttime slave catchers. South of town, just off the Baltimore Pike in the woods, old man McAllister had a mill where runaway slaves would hide in a hollow behind the water wheel. Getting back home from McAllister's Mill took Mag up the pike, into town, then back out of town to Mr. Brien's farm.

Didn't take but a few of those trips for Mag to start thinking about cutting through the woods across the pike from McAllister's to Taneytown Road, then across Cemetery Ridge, instead of staying on the roads.

One chilly autumn night in 1849, Mag shepherded a runaway coming up the Baltimore Pike to McAllister's Mill. Word had spread on the trail about Mrs. Devit's daughter, the new conductor, far more wise in her ways than her age ought to allow. McAllister waited for her at the mill as she escorted the runaway toward him.

"That old McAllister?" Mag shouted at the shadow at the end of the trail from the pike to the mill.

"Last I saw you in town you were a little girl!" McAllister shouted back, as they greeted each other with a bear hug. The runaway young man stayed back behind Mag, curious that a white man could be so welcoming to a black woman. As usual, Mag moved the slave right along.

"Get a-goin!" Mag shouted. "This here is Mr. McAllister, shake his hand." The runaway complied cautiously.

"You're safe here young fellow," McAllister announced. "Mag, wait inside for a bit." McAllister showed the slave the hiding spot under his mill wheel, should it be needed, then brought him in where Mag had taken a seat near the fire.

"You know the cut through from the pike to Taneytown Road?" McAllister asked.

"That would sure be helpful," Mag declared. "I don't like bein' on them roads this time of night." McAllister took out a paper to draw a map.

"When you walk out from the mill to the pike, cross the pike, walk north about a 100 feet, then you'll see a house on the left. Behind that house is a little trail, you can barely see it, and at night, it's almost invisible."

"Invisible sounds good to me," Mag said.

"Go behind that house..."

"Whose house is it."

"They're fine, don't worry about 'em."

"Alright, they're fine, that's all well and good, but who are they, they got names??" Mag insisted. McAllister saw what William Wright had seen; a professional, at age 14, who stared into his eyes with determination that nothing be left to chance.

"They don't want anyone to know their names, I'm afraid, Mag." Disappointed, Mag just steeled herself for the journey.

"Fine. I go behind the house, then what."

"There's a well behind that house. The trail goes

from the well, behind the house, all the way to Taneytown Road. If you stay on that trail, you'll come to the road in just a few minutes. Don't step off the trail, you'll get lost in no time."

"Stay on the trail, then there's the road."

"That's right."

"Road'll just be there, right in fronta me?"

"Can't miss it. The trail just ends into the Taneytown Road." Mag took the paper with the map McAllister just drew for her, and gave him a hug.

"Thank you very much, Mr. McAllister, this'll be a big help. Never liked the smell of things on that road." As she headed down to cross the Baltimore Pike, McAllister waved. It all went perfectly. She found the house, the well behind it, then the barely visible trail through the thick woods, landing Mag at Taneytown Road. She looked warily up and down, peering through the trees. "Still don't like the smell of this road, either," Mag whispered to herself. She briefly speed walked northward on Taneytown Road until she heard a horseman's gallop behind her, and instinctively turned left, over a stone wall, into a field. After the horseman passed by, Mag took the supreme risk of traipsing across the farmland on Cemetery Ridge between the Taneytown Road and her home over the crest of the ridge on the other side, on Emmitsburg Road. Before cresting the ridge, Mag would learn another lesson of the night, hearing a shotgun cock.

"Who goes there!?!"

Not so much startled as annoyed, Mag turned in the dark of night to see a small, ragged old farmer pointing a shotgun at her. "Who goes there!?" the farmer shouted again. It was Peter Swisher, a tenant farmer on Peter Frey's land. Mag knew all about Frey and Swisher, from the briefings Abraham Brien and Mama gave Mag in anticipation of just such an occasion.

A cosmos of thoughts crowded Mag's mind, foremost being love and a newfound awe for her Mama. Just turned 14, Mag was beautiful, just like Mama, tossing her head coyly as she stared down the barrel of Mr. Swisher's gun, shaking in his angry hands. Mag knew Mama had to have been in this pickle herself, once or twice. Was this how a white man's "innards" managed to mingle with Mama's black blood to make Mag "yellow"? Is that how Mama would get out of this jam? Or would she play it cool? Realizing she possessed both the power to seduce, and the power of information, Mag used both, instinctively.

"I beg yo' pardon??" Mag sneered, fists thrown into her hips, confidence beaming. Mag could tell Swisher was staring, shocked at Mag's beauty and daring. The shotgun came down, her first mission accomplished.

"Oh, I'm sorry miss," Swisher demurred, "I didn't

know you was a lady."

"Who you think you talkin' to??" Mag pressed. Swisher was putty in her hands.

"Apologies, miss, please, I just saw a stranger on my land, and..."

"This ain't YOUR land, is it? This ol' man Frey's land!" Swisher was speechless.

"Oh, I know, miss, I just..." The hook set, Mag went in for the kill. She took her hands off her hips, strolling toward Swisher as glamorously as she could muster.

"There, there," Mag consoled, "...now what's your name sir?"

"Swisher, ma'am, Peter Swisher, pleased to meet you, I'm just wonderin'..."

"Wonderin' WHAT?"

"Oh no, ma'am, I didn't mean to..."

The dance proceeded, Mag toying with the tired old farmer at will, finally convincing Swisher she was just on a late night delivery of some laundry, and that was that. Cresting Cemetery Ridge, not looking back, Mag heaved breath mercifully down the other side, terror finally piercing her to the bones. "Why can't Mr. Brien own that land?" she whispered to herself nervously; it would make things so much safer, easier. But the close call was averted, a lesson learned, and Mag's secret weapons revealed to her.

2 PETER MARKS

A Prussian in flight

The blood of nobility was on his hands, so Peter Marx had to run. It seemed like the thing to do at the time. Rise up, kill some nobles, the world changes, workers govern, peasants freed, prancing toffs hung by the nearest yard arm, everyone's happy. Next thing he knew, Peter was in the cargo hold of a schooner to Liverpool, 17, alone, filthy, hungry, tired, and scared.

Arrestingly handsome young Peter could smell revolution in the air of his hometown Koenigsberg in spring, 1848. It consumed the whole of Europe, like a typhoon. France, Italy, Ireland, Norway, Denmark, and every inch of German speaking ground boiled with contempt for royals and priests and anyone with a title or a robe. Another world seemed suddenly possible, even real. Peter could taste it. One day, a passing radical handed him the Communist Manifesto, written by a man with Peter's last name. Peter felt fate had chosen him, at only 16 years old.

Peter's mother begged him to stay in school. His father merely ignored the entire affair, quite certain whatever was this "revolution" nonsense would come to nothing. Then Peter would come crawling back to his studies to thank his father for being so wise and...noble. The stench of reaction, even in his own family, sickened Peter, a fuel to his wanderlust, and his growing fervor. So, off he went.

Soon, defected nobles were ordering Peter around the drill ground, and success! Overnight, Europe was new. Then, a year of hanging in the balance dragged on. As the swashbuckling charm wore off, revolutions across Europe bogged down in division and counter insurgency. The next spring, as suddenly as it began, it was all crushed. Nobility had won. Peter's father was right. It came to nothing. No rage would ever again grip Peter so fully. There was no returning.

Peter found himself in the remnant revolutionary army fleeing for its life across the Swiss border. Over his year rising up, Peter got too close to his comrades in arms he'd watched die, or flee, disappearing from his world like phantoms who were never there in the first place. When a revolution dies out, the heaviest remainder is the loneliness, and Peter was oh so alone, all of a sudden.

And on the run. With the wrong last name. He would be hunted until a noose or firing squad brought him to his end. A well-worn underground trail of comrades smuggled Peter from the Swiss mountains through France, to the port in Calais. Peter never forgot walking up the ramp for a British boat to Liverpool, the longest seconds of his life, trying to decide what name to give for the passengers log. What would happen when they heard his last name? As luck would have it, there was a long line; more time to think it over. To avoid speaking, thus revealing his German accent, he took out a slip of paper to write a name to hand to the porter. There, and then, he became Peter Marks, the pencil hesitating as he wrote unfamiliar letters onto the end of his name.

The First Ghost of Gettysburg finds Peter

Upon leaving Liverpool's docks with his new last name and only the tattered revolutionary peasant clothes on his back, Peter Marks thought he'd descended into hell. The dust of slave-harvested cotton thickened the air like summer pollen, sticking to his cotton clothes, agents scurrying about buying and selling men's souls by the baleful, everyone covered in it. In no time, Peter's mouth caked with fuzz as he walked ever more angrily into a city of Mammon Himself.

Topping it all off was the rancid stench. Smokestacks belched choking sulfurous billows, streets bubbled with gutters of human waste, rotting fish heads and produce, ladies' flowing skirts stained to black at their edges. Peasant impoverished Prussia was a Garden of Eden compared to industrial revolution English citics. Fate seemed to rub capitalism's victory over Peter's "revolution" in his face, literally.

Peter just kept walking, suddenly nostalgic for the frenzied farcically chaotic retreat with his comrades, into mountains where he could at least breathe. He had to get out. Mercifully it began to rain. Harder, Peter begged the sky, mouth open to it, please rain harder so I can wash the cotton dust out of my throat. Peter marched ever faster, past slums, factories, his pace quickening in desperation just to get to anywhere else.

Liverpool's outskirts gave way to English countryside, fresh air returning to Peter's lungs, finally affording the luxury to slow down, to rest. He sat near a country pub on the road to Manchester, using the rain in vain attempts to scrub the cotton dust off. Finally, he could think. What to do now? Carriages passed by the pub, stopping to drop off and pick up gentlemen in fine dress.

Fine dress. An idea occurred, cheering Peter instantly.

Having grown up among them, Peter knew the rich. All he needed was to find one who took pity. Peter studied the pub's patrons coming and going, deciding these rich weren't rich enough. A longer march was required; something Peter was quite used to. Resigned to a night outside, sleep being a mere potential, Peter got up, gave the cotton dust one last useless brush to try and wad it away, then walked again. English weather came and went, embedding the cotton dust further into his clothes, when a stroke of luck seemed to break in Peter's favor.

A suitcase fell off a passing carriage, which kept going, rounding a bend oblivious. Peter looked both ways to make sure no one cared, then ran into the road, grabbed the suitcase, and rushed behind a hedgerow, opening the case to find a gentlemanly wardrobe. Into the case went the revolutionary clothes he last put on somewhere in Switzerland. Peter became a Prussian gentleman again, if slightly ill-fitted, carrying his former uprisen self in a found, fine leather bag. There was even a hat and ascot. Off he went, a spring now in his step, the handiwork of The First Ghost of Gettysburg.

It was a mischievous thing, this ghost, like rock and roll. It was nowhere, and everywhere. From it proceeded every pitiable ghost of Gettysburg past, present, and future, alive, dead, or undead; the first and master of them all, conjuring them into being at will, or casting them to oblivion. A trickster, the First Ghost of Gettysburg was alternately playful, cruel, malevolent, tender, everything in between then beyond.

Neither time nor space bound The First Ghost of Gettysburg. Immeasurable, but all consuming, it was eternal, yet nonexistent. It was, then wasn't. It could wield the power of all the suns of the universe, or be as gentle as the breeze of a butterfly's wings. It was both angry and loving, laughing and crying, dancing and paralyzed, together.

Possessing this duality doomed a timeless torment unimaginable onto the Ghost, for it simply could not be one or the other. It was both, in equal measure, always. Thus was The First Ghost of Gettysburg cursed to wander time seeking resolution, peace, and rest, which never came. Forever destined to conflict with itself, between the greatest powers of the cosmos within it, The First Ghost of Gettysburg was a wretched thing.

It moved imperceptibly within souls yet living. It could be a notion, a thought, a nightmare or a dream, a glimpse, a turned head, the wave of a hand, an intense heat welling up suddenly or an icy chill descending never to depart, like death. The living never knew it was this Ghost, The First of Gettysburg, which seized them at will, unannounced, for this ghost was present only in silence. Not a sound.

In this silence the Ghost's tormented conflict performed its passion play. The longer the quiet, the deeper the hell, the Ghost's fangs slowly unsheathed, dripping with its own bloody drool, unseen sinking unheard through the living flesh slowly, in the quiet. Deep silence so total one rushed to fill it, with anything at all; your breath, a drop of a stick, the rustle of leaves, a scream. Anything to dispatch the Ghost's cursed nothingness, its torment so unspeakable the only noise was made through its victims, the living, through whom the Ghost's eternal yin then yang would manifest in life. That day in 1849, the Ghost came across Peter Marks, to toss his new clothes at him on the road.

Cotton dusted stench of Liverpool behind him, Peter blissfully wandered the rolling English countryside eastward, inland, forgetting his troubles, getting lost, jaunty in his found upper class haberdashery. Disembarked at sunrise in exile, that afternoon he crossed the Mersey into Cheshire before realizing dusk approached. Time to find that just-rich-enough rube to dupe into giving him a bed for the night. At a crossroads of country lanes between Liverpool and Manchester, The Ghost breathed Peter's first step on the road to Gettysburg, a cool breeze turning Peter's head to see a gardener clipping a hedgerow in the dusk.

The gardener caught sight of Peter, stopping his hedge clipping to study Peter's approach. Peter wondered as he came closer to the gardener, should he speak German or English? The gardener waved, a short portly fellow, middle-aged, obviously a laborer. "Good evening, milord!" the gardener shouted. Peter smiled gentlemanly, nodded. Peter decided his language for the encounter.

"Sprechen sie Deutsch?" The gardener dropped his clipper, gasping, demonstratively.

"You don't say?? Well, we haven't had one of your lot at Arley in years! Quite sorry old boy, I hope you understand English!" Peter was relieved; he could listen, but needn't speak.

"Milord," Peter bowed, tipping the top hat he'd found in the street, wondering if the gardener could smell the odor seeping up his collar out the ascot into his own nose; he hadn't had a bath in weeks.

"Bipkins at your service, old boy! Such terrible news from Westphalia! Bloody reds. Come, I shall walk you to the house. Bipkins it is!"

Peter cast his eyes about the lush lane, soaking information in, suddenly unable to ignore his own filth. Bipkins babbled constantly. "Just a tenant here, milord, keeping the hedges tidy, mind you. But I'll take you to His Lordship, I will!" Bipkins seemed to have mistaken Peter for some sort of German nobility related to whoever His Lordship was. Peter couldn't believe his luck.

"A sight to see, you are! What tales of terror you must have, I say! We thought you were all dead!" And on. And on...Peter tossed in an occasional nod, "ja", "danke"...his mind racing with options and risks.

"Are Lady Warburton's cousins alright?? Bloody reds. No respect for dignity, for honor! Honor I say!" They turned a corner into the courtyard, the towering glory of Rowland Egerton-Warburton's brand new, just rebuilt Arley Hall stunning Peter.

"Wait here, good man, it's dinner time, but I'll find the butler I will!" Bipkins left Peter in the courtyard, bewildered, gazing at the estate, smelling himself. Now what? Who was he now? Peter had to think fast.

Bipkins and a tuxedoed butler rushed out into the dusky courtyard. Looking every bit the well pressed and starched oldest of English money on earth, the butler marched aggressively toward Peter, examining him up and down as he approached. Peter tipped his hat again, and Bipkins was off, shouting "Cheerio!" Peter thanked heaven for the found upper class clothes.

"Welcome to Arley Hall my good man, His Lordship is at dinner, come in, we will warm you up." Like an invisible ooze, the odor of Peter's journey into exile crawled into his nostrils. But he had a bed for the night, and yet another new identity. Just who was he mistaken to be? Peter would let his new hosts decide that for him.

Peter settles into footmanry

Leaving Arley Hall for mass at Great Budworth one late autumn Sunday morning, Lord and Lady Warburton finally noticed the new footman, Peter. Her Ladyship dropped her hat while stepping into the coach, Peter picked it up, dusted it off, smiled, then bowing, handed it to Her Ladyship. Since Bipkins ushered him in that summer, Peter had been a footman long enough such that his first direct encounter with the masters of the house was effortless.

"I dare say, milord," Lady Warburton said to her husband as Peter closed the coach door, "Arley Hall boasts the most handsome footmen in the whole of Cheshire!" As the coach galloped off to church, the Marxist rebel in disguise turned on his heel, back inside to polish some silver.

By November, 1849, the new footman whose Deutschland masters had been tragically run out of their Westphalia castle by those filthy reds (or so Peter let everyone believe) had become Arley Hall's most dashing and quietly mysterious newcomer. Ears ever alert, Peter absorbed all an overhearing footman could hope to know about the German relatives of His Lordship, who Peter was assumed to have heroically tried to save from the reds, before being hounded across borders, mountains, over the sea, to wander into the welcoming arms of the

English cousins. Without a peep crossing his lips, Peter's presence was explained, accepted, internalized by all, creating Peter's new world for him, by mere leap to conclusion of the landed gentry English mind. Every day, Peter pinched himself to see if it all was real.

Peter's room in the basement of Arley Hall was tiny, but brand new like the rest of the massive country house Lord Warburton had built from scratch, having tired of the 200 year old rotting carcass the family seat had become. Traced back at least to the 12th century, the family Peter fell into was precisely the sort he'd left behind in Prussia to destroy; very like his own. The irony of it all would consume Peter tortuously, eventually. But for now, it would do, if only for the rest he so desperately needed after his year marching across Europe in revolutionary rags. Even the routine of his workday felt like repose, Peter's dreamlike respite in footmanry affording a calmness to soak in his new surroundings, brush up his English, to think, and to sleep in an honest to goodness, warm bed.

The most "work" to do was on oneself. His fellow footmen, the oldest barely 22, prided themselves on appearance and good looks, all day admiring each other's boyish beauty, adjusting each other's collars, bow ties, competing for the shiniest shoes, the most well coiffed hair and pressed tuxedo. But Peter stood out, being all at once not English, not talkative, not bothered by much of anything, and cloaked in intrigue. His year amongst the rabble of young men who made up the reddest of the red radicals of Europe had taught Peter his looks and demeanor carried much weight, and would turn the heads of both women and men alike. After a few months being stared at in the fishbowl of footmanry at Arley Hall, 17-year-old Peter accepted it was indeed possible to be too handsome.

On a misty, chilly autumnal Saturday day off, Peter wandered to the village of Great Budworth, part of the estate, for a pint or two in the George & Dragon pub, and there was Bipkins. Greeting each other as long lost friends, night closed over the pub as they holed up in a warm corner, tentatively. Peter sensed a distance Bipkins kept, becoming curious. Something was up, and had been up, since they met along the hedgerow months ago. Bipkins sensed Peter had figured things out, looked around sheepishly, then leaning over their pints across the table, he cut to the chase.

"I know you didn't work for the German cousins at the castle in Westphalia, old boy," Bipkins whispered. "I just let them think so, because...well...you looked like you needed a break." Peter stared into Bipkins' suddenly steely glare. "Smelled like it, too."

Peter smiled, and sipped his beer, still refusing to give up the game. Bipkins winked, letting the game proceed, then shouted to the bar, "Two more!" The night grew raucous and lively, both stumbling out at closing time, Peter still playing the game, Bipkins letting him.

"You just stay at Arley Hall as long as you can," Bipkins slurred, catching himself to stop slurring just enough to be deadly serious. "When you need to move on, you find me."

Peter falls in love with a footman

Autumn passed to winter at Arley Hall, Peter fitting in, becoming an expert, rising in stature among the country house's staff, swiftly respected for his ease among the upper class he grew up in, which only a year and a half ago he'd sworn to destroy. Of course, footmanry at Arley Hall afforded Peter no outlet for the radical he once was, but for one. In January, 1850, Peter fell in love with a fellow footman, Paul. The double entendre of their two names together made the affair's secrecy extra delightful.

Peter's only love his entire 17 years was revolution. Being exceptionally handsome, sex presented itself to Peter constantly, gender being no matter. Peter took whatever came, but love he did not know. He did know that upper class sexual exploitation of the help, and their own young, was no secret. It sickened Peter his entire childhood, fanning his radical flames. Marching across Europe in revolutionary rags, Peter and his comrades made regular mockery of the bourgeois feeding upon the proletariat's helpless, yet oh so attractive serfs &

servants. So, immediately upon his escort into Arley Hall by the mysterious Bipkins, Peter, being adorably beautiful, was fully aware advances were imminent from His Lordship, or whatever duke, duchess or dame might use their position of power to satiate themselves upon him. It came with the territory, always. Thus, Paul caught Peter's eye.

Both teenagers, Paul was impossibly more adorable than Peter, blonde to Peter's brunette, blue eyes to Peter's brown, a bit younger and smaller, so Peter kept watch over his fellow footman. At first, Paul was merely Peter's useful early warning system, a case study in how the approach from power toward their exploited would proceed. Soon, Peter felt a big brother attachment to Paul, and began looking out for him. They would catch each other's eyes serving the soup course at dinner, or while loading a coach, knowing glances between the soon to be preyed upon turned slowly into longer moments of another sort, the way puppy love always grows.

That January, a dinner was held for Her Ladyship's Something Or Other Occasion, a kind of post-Christmas minor league cattle call for the lesser cousins, uncles, aunts who didn't make the cut for the high holidays' full Arley Hall treatment. Peter knew this lot would be on the hunt, so was on high alert when some groping drunk third uncle thrice removed began orbiting Paul all night. It all happened in a flash.

About midnight, three sheets to the breeze, Uncle

Alfred cornered the littler Paul in a hallway, looming over him under the pretense of Paul having failed to cross some "t" or dot some "i" whilst serving the pickled herring or whatever, hoping to falsely extort a dalliance upstairs. Peter swooped in just in the nick of time, assuming authority he did not have, stepping between them. Paul heaved a sigh of relief.

"Do allow me to handle this matter, Uncle Alfred," Peter declared. The drunken uncle withdrew, Peter watching him like a hawk until he stumbled out of sight. Then, Peter turned to Paul, who could not believe what had just occurred. A stare. Peter pretended to reprimand, with a hand on Paul's shoulder. "You alright?" Peter asked Paul, then both smiled an uncomfortably long moment, melting each other.

Being the older one, the next morning, it was Peter who took charge of making sure no one knew he'd stayed the night in Paul's servants' quarters. Around the breakfast table, serving eggs to hungover Uncle Alfred and the gathered bottom tier glitterati, Peter & Paul's glances transformed, far more knowing, longer, deeper, as another layer of double life enveloped Peter, another time bomb began to tick. But now, for the first time, Peter knew love.

Gossip being what it was at Arley Hall, hiding their footman love affair was never going to last for Peter and Paul. Servants' quarters buzzed constantly; who was with whom, which lord or lady was preying upon which of the help at which hour. Within a month, Peter began to fear the walls closing in. Paul never did.

Ever youthfully oblivious to consequence, Paul far too often left clues to be observed. A lingered stare across the drawing room, or a smile toward Peter when a footman ought not to, Paul was the young lover everyone dreams of, wishes for. He joyfully worshipped the ground Peter trod upon, utterly unable to hide it. Peter remembered being that way himself at that age not very long ago (about a girl, once), so he reveled in Paul's adoration, returning it only carefully, out of sight. Though he considered it often, Peter never had the heart to tell Paul to cool it, until one day, Paul was gone.

Peter entered the servants' kitchen that February morning to see Paul's chair empty at the breakfast table. Instantly, he knew. His heart stopped then began to pound, he lost his breath, fingers twitched. Taking his seat in slow motion, his blood ran like hot lead, heavy and burning, sinking into the chair as if the earth swallowed him whole. Another layer of Peter's doubled, tripled life folded upon itself to multiply its dead weight onto Peter's soul. He groped for the spoon next to his bowl of porridge, found it, twirled it, each moment now an eternity, as the servants ate.

Curtain up, the performance commenced. No change, Peter's mind demanded, as his heart broke, eyes welled up, stomach knotted. *You do not care where Paul has gone, you mustn't. Not ever. An empty seat at this breakfast table is a fact of life in a great house servants' quarters, you bloody fool. They come and they go. No one asks any questions, and you will not now. Eat your fucking meal, not a god damned peep.*

So he ate, each spoonful harder to swallow. Paul's empty chair in Peter's peripheral vision seemed a stone in a graveyard, none mourning over it, just a bunch of useless indentured serfs scraping their bowls like vultures for one last bit of gruel graciously afforded by their masters, spoons clanking, none daring to look up, around, or at each other. Time bent.

Prison. They handed him over to the constable. I'm next. Which of the snakes at this table blew our cover? Maybe we'll be in the same jail? No, they'll send me someplace worse. Paul will die there. He's a sitting duck. Why did I ever come here? It's all my fault. Peter groped for air, trying so hard not to move his face shook, silence so total he heard a tear drop from his cheek to the table, thumping into the soft wood, when finally, someone broke the spell racing to sit in the empty chair.

"Don't cry, Peter," Paul said, sitting down like an angel from the sky. "This morning's porridge can't be *that* bad, is it?"

Peter looked up from the bowl, and there was Paul, perfection in his footman tuxedo, just a bit late today. Embarrassed relief beyond measure engulfed Peter, delivering him into Paul's usual morning smile, lost in his eyes for a moment that lasted a lifetime.

Then, to work after breakfast, a dozen or so carriages arriving to join the lord of the house for some grand lunch whatever, god knows. When the last ghoulish gentry were safely up the walk, Paul, as usual, stole a moment at the end of the courtyard with Peter; just another, little smile, bright as a dove.

Peter decided. It might break Paul's heart, but Peter would do what he must to keep their little world separate from every other world around them. It had to be done. A gossiping gaggle of the arriving gentlemen's wives heading into the house caught Peter and Paul's moment, then stared at the boys, suspiciously, before entering, all atwitter. Peter, of course, felt it. Turning to stare ramrod straight into the vast Arley estate, Peter whispered what only Paul would hear, being so...too, close by.

"We have to talk."

3 MILLIE OF MANY MUSICS

A fiddler arrives in St. Paul

A s Peter Marks swashbuckled his way across Europe to a new last name and a romance at a country house, a tiny girl named Millie was well on her way to mastering the fine art of unassuming diplomacy on America's frontier. Millie was born in 1841 on the prairie near the pioneer fur trading village on the Mississippi River called Pig's Eye, soon to change its own name to St. Paul, mercifully. Millie's father was a fur trading Québécois, who married, purely for business, the product of a Dakota mother and Irish fur trading father. Fur trading was much easier if you could count a Dakota as a relative.

Thus, little Millie was a quilt of languages by age 6

when missionary teacher Harriet Bishop opened the first school in St. Paul in 1847. Sung to sleep by Mama's Irish reels, mastering French just to keep her papa's attention, playing with the Dakota children who always seemed to be around, Millie was a sponge from the moment she entered the world. The new school's children, a tower of Babel of tongues, presented Yankee lady Bishop with a problem she hadn't expected.

Miss Bishop didn't know, but it wasn't her translator from nearby Fort Snelling who kept the lid on things at the new log cabin schoolhouse. Small, plain looking 6-year-old Millie did, who, with one breath, could bridge any language gap in the room. Millie learned not to make a show of it by watching how the stern missionary Miss Bishop treated her translator, as a thing to be used to accomplish what Miss Bishop simply could not. "Shy", they called Millie, which suited Millie just fine. By autumn, 1848, Miss Bishop's school most taught Millie she didn't much like missionaries. St. Paul was already filled with saloons and taverns, and Miss Bishop never failed to rail against the demon drink to the children. To Millie, it sounded personal, because Papa always brought back a song from the taverns. Singing with Papa was another way to keep his attention whenever he was around; fur trading kept Papa so far away half the year, off in the wilderness.

Winter arrived. St. Paul was a lonely place when the river iced over; nothing, and no one, came or went.

Everything just stood in place. So, during the brutally cold winter of 1848 to 1849, Millie worked hard on Papa's fiddle. No one knew why Papa, being French, kept that thing, except that it came in barter from an Irishman, thus thought valuable. All the previous autumn, Millie spent days trying her hand at it, eeking out melodies. Upon hearing the screeches and sour notes, the Dakota children named her "Millie of Many Musics". Took Millie a while to coax anything resembling music out of that fiddle, but being just another language, music came easily.

Millie couldn't wait for the river to thaw, so she could play the fiddle at the landing to welcome whoever came off the boats. The March day the ice on the river cracked began a new daily St. Paul ritual. A crowd gathered at the landing every afternoon. Nothing happened. The crowd went home to bed. The next day, the crowd came back, etc. Two weeks this went on. Every day those two weeks, joining just about everyone, Papa went into town. The wait ended April 9, 1849. That Monday, Millie insisted she join Papa this time, with the fiddle. Her younger brothers chimed in, suddenly wanting to go, too. At 8 years old, Millie was a bit of an instigator. "Eat your breakfast," Mama ordered them all, trying to change the subject.

"But I want to play for the first steamer!" Millie declared. Big news would be on that first steamer of 1849. Over winter, the U.S. Congress considered legislation officially making Minnesota a U.S. territory, the first step toward statehood, the delegation sent down river on the last steamboat of 1848. Everyone in St. Paul knew the next steamboat would bring the result, good or bad. No one in St. Paul had any inkling of the flood of immigrants that would join the news off those boats that spring, and for years thereafter.

Papa looked at Mama with a resigned grin. "It's you Irish," Papa sneered with love. "You put that minstrel in her, ce n'est pas moi!" It was decided. Millie would play at the landing that afternoon, steamboat or not. The other kids moped, knowing they'd be left home. Being the first born, Millie was always the favorite. Millie burst with excitement all day, practicing Papa's fiddle to brush up her first tune, the Irish lullaby Mama sang her to sleep with since she was born. Papa hated it.

"It's too sad for such an occasion," Papa explained to Millie on the wagon into town. "We need to teach you more songs." As storm clouds gathered to bring a torrential downpour, Millie couldn't care less what news the steamboat would bring. Papa wanted Millie to learn more songs, that's all that mattered. The sadness of her repertoire couldn't match Millie's sadness when the rains began. Papa never saw Millie so disappointed as when he put the fiddle in the box under the wagon seat after the clouds opened a spring deluge upon St. Paul. To cheer her up, Papa carried Millie on his shoulders into town, like he did since she was a baby. Standing under an

American flag stuck onto the wall of the one general store in St. Paul, they heard a steamboat whistle.

"Grab that flag!" Papa shouted, and off with a sprint they joined the throng headed to the landing, persistent whistling from the steamboat convincing all the news was here, and the best kind. As what seemed to be the whole town swarmed onto the decks of the *Doctor Franklin*, news of Minnesota becoming a territory didn't so much arrive in St. Paul as was seized that Monday.

Waving the American flag on Papa's shoulders, soaked to her bones, Millie fixed her gaze on an old man, a fiddler, playing the Star Spangled Banner for the delirious revelers on the decks of the *Doctor Franklin*. First, she was jealous; he played so well, he seemed like an angel. Then, she noticed a little boy following the fiddler around the deck taking tips into his hat from the crowd gleefully generous with their coins. As they disembarked, the old man's fiddle went into a case away from the rain as he and the boy followed the crowd off the steamboat, passing by carrying suitcases. Soaked to her bones but the happiest little girl in St. Paul, Millie would remember that Monday the rest of her life.

Millie meets the Dooleys

Papa's weary ears led to a quest. Independence

Day, 1849, Millie's father had one priority at the parade in the suddenly bustling little town. Find that fiddler who got off the first boat of spring, and beg him to teach Millie to play. His sanity demanded it. Mama thought music lessons an extravagance. Papa's ears considered the matter an emergency. "She needs to learn WHERE to put her FINGERS on those strings!" Papa would yell. Every. Single. Day.

Just where a fiddler with a little boy might end up after arriving on a steamboat was anyone's guess. St. Paul was the final stop on the north end of the Mississippi River. From there, a man could disappear into a continent. Now that Minnesota was officially a territory of the United States, immigrants spread out from that steamboat landing in every direction. That fiddler could be a traveling minstrel, touring every trading post on the plains, finding a home anywhere. Minnesota's first July 4th celebration ever was sure to muster every soul of the mere 1,000 in the territory, wherever they might wander the rest of the year. It was Papa's only shot.

He had a cunning plan. Trundling into town with the family, Papa parked the wagon on the end of Third Street, guiding the family to a spot near where the parade would pass. Papa banked on the fiddler joining the parade with some brass marching band, or something; a total crap shoot. Desperation tends to force such gambles. As Mama and her brothers milled about town, Papa and an ever so excited Millie sat together as the parade marched by, staring at everyone with an eagle eye.

"After today, Millie, *mon dieu*, you and that fiddle...*quelle beau musique!*"

"What if we can't find him?" Millie wondered.

"Shhhh Millie! Listen!" Sweet deliverance approached. Papa and Millie sprang from the ground to see, bringing up the rear of the parade, the fiddler and his boy with the hat collecting tips. Papa let them march by as Millie stared in awe at the fiddler playing a mixture of the Star Spangled Banner and...something magical. "Allons," Papa barked, grabbing Millie by the hand to follow the parade. Millie's heart raced, imagining herself playing in the parade someday, as Papa kept a steely eye on his quarry, dreaming of relief.

The parade gathered for the usual endless speechifying, as the fiddler and his boy wandered to the American House hotel to rest on the stoop of Mr. H. M. Rice's brand new white clapboard hostelry, teeming with new arrivals to St. Paul. The boy counted the tips from his hat, as Papa and Millie approached.

"Bonjour, monsieur," Papa said tipping his hat. The fiddler looked up from the stoop with the weary eyes of a soul merely existing.

"Happy Independence Day!" the fiddler declared, perking up. "Paddy Dooley at your service, my nephew here, Seamus." Millie turned to Seamus to smile a hello, and was immediately smitten. Seamus kept counting the tips, oblivious. Millie at eight years old still thought boys icky. Seamus would be the first to change that.

"I am Pierre Richard, this is Millie my daughter. Would you mind Millie borrowing your fiddle for a moment?" Mr. Dooley understood immediately, handing Millie his bow and violin. Millie played Mama's Irish lullaby nervously, flat, as usual. Seamus finally looked up from the tips in his hat and smirked, shaking his head. Millie noticed Seamus' smirk, his red hair rustle with his head shaking, all of which made her playing worse. When Millie finished, slightly embarrassed, Mr. Dooley deployed positive reinforcement.

"That is my mother's old favorite," Mr. Dooley delighted. "We are from Ireland."

"Can you teach my daughter to play what you were just playing? What was it?"

"Schubert, Vivaldi, a little this and that for the holiday."

Millie finally chimed in. "You must be the finest fiddler of Ireland!"

A short negotiation later, Papa's quest was fulfilled, and the Dooleys' rent for the American House hotel paid until Millie could learn Schubert. "Go upstairs and get the sheet music," Mr. Dooley instructed Seamus, who was off with a flash, Millie running into the hotel behind him, Papa left behind with Mr. Dooley, smiling at each other. Papa's relief could not be contained.

"You have no idea how happy you've made me....us."

Millie never heard Seamus speak until after school one day that autumn of 1849. At monthly violin lessons in Mr. Dooley's room at the America House hotel, Seamus just sat in a corner reading, or stood at the window staring outside while his Uncle Paddy taught Millie for an hour or two. She had trouble keeping her eyes off Seamus; something about him.

Millie couldn't know Seamus was the last of his line of Dooleys in Ireland, his entire family having perished in the great famine. His Uncle Paddy, who dabbled in the nationalist movement born of the famine, kept Seamus alive until both had to make the great crossing to America, penniless and emaciated. All Millie could tell was that something terrible weighed upon Seamus, less a 9-year-old boy than a specter of anger and sadness together, withdrawn into a low boil of silence. After Seamus' first few months in St. Paul, Millie noticed he wasn't so bony anymore, healthier on the outside, but inside, an untold story she was dying to know.

At Miss Bishop's little schoolhouse in fall 1849, Seamus was barely visible amongst the crowded mosaic of kids; the Dakotas, the Ojibwe, the French, the Yankees, and the newest arrivals, the Germans, who would soon practically outnumber everyone. Seamus having sparked Milile's first stirrings of a crush on a boy, she looked out for the newcomer kid from Ireland who never made a peep. Her diplomacy skills sharpening by the day, Millie could tell trouble would soon find Seamus, which it did, one day as school let out.

When a group of boys teased Seamus for being "mute", Seamus uttered the first words Millie had ever heard from him. "Shut up, half breed", and the fight was on. Seamus flew into a flurry of punches this way and that, soon over matched by the "half breeds". Tension between Dakotas and the settlers always just below the surface in St. Paul, Millie knew where things could lead, so stepped in. It was all over in less than a minute, Millie's mere words casting violence to the wind. The "half breeds" already knew and loved Millie, so if she said enough, that was enough.

Millie rushed to Seamus on the ground, his lip bleeding, his beautiful red hair covered with dirt, her heart jumping. "Are you ok??" Millie shouted, bending down to help him up. Seamus paused on the ground, their eyes met, and Millie saw his heart open then slam shut in the blink of his watery eyes. The silence returned. Millie would not have it this time, having just saved Seamus from sparking a border war, becoming indignant. "You could say thank you, you know."

"I don't need no help from no half breed girl," Seamus spit out. Millie chuckled.

"I beg your pardon, but you sure needed my help just now!" Finally the ice broke, and Seamus smiled for the first time since he arrived in St. Paul. Millie helped him up, a schoolyard brawl sparking a stormy lifelong courtship.

The First Ghost of Gettysburg visits Millie & Seamus

Knowing no time nor space, the Ghost chose a blizzard in January, 1850, to visit St. Paul's new American House hotel, crammed with immigrants, where in winter, Millie stayed the night at Mr. Dooley's room for her monthly violin lesson. The Ghost swooped down as Millie listened to Mr. Dooley play Vivaldi's "Winter" at the end of the lesson, using the first bars to demonstrate the difference between major and minor key. The Ghost haunted the spaces between such things, best.

"There, you see?" Mr. Dooley taught, as his little nephew Seamus stared out the window at the blinding snowstorm.

"Please keep playing, Mr. Dooley," Millie asked, almost begging. Something within her, the Ghost of course, chilled her to the bone. The music was warming, it must continue. Mr. Dooley obliged, Millie closed her eyes, soaring into the tiny hotel room's corners on Italian baroque played by an Irishman. Mr. Dooley paused, crashing Millie out of comfort, her eyes ripped open, staring at the ceiling, the Ghost seizing her. Seamus seemed to notice, his head snapping from the window to look at Millie, fearful wonder in his eyes. Instinctively Millie grabbed her violin.

"May I try??" and off she went, eyes fixed at the sheet music, the rhythmic first notes bouncing off the strings out her bow as Mr. Dooley accompanied with the difficult solo. Seamus turned from the window of snow in awe. The Ghost was putting on a command performance for the tiny room. Before she knew it, the Ghost had gone, leaving Millie standing with her violin, sweating, heaving, Mr. Dooley amazed at the child prodigy before him.

"Why does minor key sound so sad?" Millie asked urgently.

"It is like life," Mr. Dooley answered, folding the sheet music away. "It makes the major keys sound happier." Millie finally relaxed. It was bedtime. Mr. Dooley curled up with Seamus on the floor, leaving Millie to the bed, unable to sleep at all. She heard Seamus weep, calling for his parents long gone, Uncle Paddy comforting the boy constantly. The Ghost took pity on them, returning briefly in the blowing snow outside to whisper Millie away with the wind, and help Seamus cry himself to sleep.

It was the famine. Seamus' uncle Paddy, Mr.

Dooley, never told Millie the whole story during violin lessons, just enough to know Seamus was the last survivor of his entire family to make it across the ocean. Seamus would let out clues for Millie, bursting out in unpredictable violent fury, constantly, a shriek of hate here, a muttering under his breath there. He trusted no one, craved conflict, seemed bent on revenge of any kind, anywhere, anytime, extracted from anyone. Seamus held special antipathy for the "half breeds" all over St. Paul, but anyone other than Irish bore his incandescent disgust, simmering under the surface, until bedtime, when it came out in tears.

By February, 1850, the damage little 9-year-old Seamus carried with him all the way from Ireland was so clear Millie never wanted to see him again. Every day at school, Seamus ended up in some fight, punished in the corner of Miss Bishop's schoolhouse, then bolting home. Despite being his only friend in school, Millie began to dread the monthly violin lessons at Mr. Dooley's room in the America House hotel in town, because Seamus would be there. Then one day he slept over.

Away from St. Paul fiddling songs for a boozy night of military brass at Fort Snelling, Mr. Dooley arranged for Seamus to walk home from school with Millie and her brothers. With Papa out on the plain fur trapping, the meager farmhouse was bedlam, Millie's little brothers tossing kindling at the fire within Seamus, ceaselessly teasing and rough housing. As usual, Millie tried to calm things, but kids are kids, and Mama was just happy all the racing around kept them warm in the drafty cabin battered by winds howling across the plain.

As bedtime fell, Millie's mom put her foot down to get them all to bed. Millie shared Mama and Papa's bed with Seamus, her two brothers in the other. As Mama tucked Seamus in last, crawling between the guest and Millie to settle down, Seamus seemed to suddenly realize Mama was one of those "half breeds", whose bed he was expected to share.

It was over in a heartbeat. "Get off me!!" Seamus shouted, punching at Mama, his screams so terrifying Millie's brothers froze in the opposite bed, Millie cowering into the wall to escape Seamus throwing his fists. Mama grabbed and held Seamus tightly as he flailed at her, taking the blows until they slowed, Seamus weeping like an infant. Mama rocked him back and forth. "There, there, young man."

Seamus cried so hard he shivered himself to exhaustion in Mama's arms as she rocked him, whispering, "There, there." His whimpers gave way to sniffling as Seamus calmed. Mama wiped his tears, and finally, Seamus fell to sleep on her shoulder. Mama just kept rocking. Millie was amazed. As Mama curled up between them, she pulled the covers over Seamus, rolling over toward Millie to smile at her.

"What's wrong with him?" Millie asked, Seamus

breathing hard in slumber.

"Nothing a little love can't help," Mama replied, snuggling Millie away from the cold, as the gales whistled around them.

Millie tours St. Paul's saloons

Pioneer fever of every variety had ballooned St. Paul into a boomtown by summer, 1857. Hundreds of immigrants arrived by steamboat every week; Germans, Irish, and Yankee speculators dreaming of riches. Some instantly saddled up for the prairie westward, or sucked themselves into land speculation on every point of the compass. In town, streets appeared, general stores popped up, newspapers multiplied, churches consecrated, families begun, hotels and homes built, businesses established, all the trappings of society mushrooming St. Paul into an actual place, a frontier jewel at the top of the Mississippi River. Most obviously were the saloons, which were countless, dominated by German and Irish ownership. In their nightly embrace, a distinct St. Paul culture began to grow, where Millie's violin found its first voice.

By 16 years old in 1857, Millie had become one of the finest musicians in the whole of Minnesota territory, in private. Only the family's prairie cabin was filled with practices and performances. She wasn't just a fiddler, oh no, Paddy Dooley made sure of that. Papa burst with such pride in his little girl, as soon as Mama could be convinced to allow it, he introduced Millie to the saloons that summer. An instant sensation among the fortune seeking, boozing crowds, they showered her with applause and money, making Millie a bread winner for the family such that Papa even retired from fur trapping. Time with her father at the saloons was a dream come true for Millie. Miss Bishop's schoolhouse temperance lectures were long forgotten, fiddled away to oblivion sometimes five nights a week, as Papa reveled in his daughter over a delightful array of German lagers and Irish whiskeys now flowing like the river through St. Paul.

Seamus Dooley tagged along to listen to Millie whenever she played an Irish saloon. He'd grown up the same withdrawn 17-year-old he was at 8 when he arrived on the *Doctor Franklin* with Uncle Paddy, boyishly handsome, still a bit short, but wiry strong. Millie couldn't help but notice; that red hair, that pouty disposition, never failed to catch her eye. Their odd detached courtship had been underway for years, Millie's protective nature the only thing Seamus could count on besides his uncle. Millie's parents assumed they'd wed someday, frontier marriages being most often of necessity and convenience of proximity. As a husband, he would do. Seamus easily found income amidst the land speculators who needed newly drawn plots cleared, or the wood sellers refueling the steamboats crowding the river, sometimes a dozen or more waiting daily to fuel up. His whole childhood, land prices never fell. Like so many in St. Paul by 1857, Seamus couldn't resist speculating with his hard earned wages in a variety of schemes, much to Uncle Paddy's dismay. Quite the opposite, Millie took every cent tossed into her violin case home to the cabin, where Mama watched over it in a box.

At the saloons, Seamus let his Irish out. Imminent brawling usually closed Millie's performance if Seamus were there. He'd lose himself in her music at first, then the liquor worked its magic, leading Seamus first to joy, then to melancholy, then to anger, like clockwork. Millie learned not to play Irish songs until the end of the evening if Seamus were there. They'd send Seamus to the dark place, then she'd have to break up whatever Seamus exploded, as she did that day in Miss Bishop's schoolyard when they were little, sparing Minnesota a border war sparked by Seamus fighting with the Dakota kids. Worked every time. Before a single saloon drenched punch got thrown, Millie deployed a diplomatic word or two, then Drunk Seamus would collapse in shame and tears into Millie's embrace, then, the show over, Papa would walk Seamus home to Mr. Dooley's. An odd courtship, indeed.

Finally, one warm night that spring, they kissed. Millie and Papa were getting settled at Henry Shearn's Head Quarters II saloon when Seamus swooped in filled with excitement. Millie had never seen Seamus so happy, if happy ever. It was intoxicating. "First round's on me!" Seamus shouted at Mr. Shearn behind the bar. She rushed to him, insatiably curious.

"What has gotten into you??" Millie demanded, delighted by this new Seamus.

"Millie, we can be married now."

"Married??" The prospect had always hovered between them, but hearing it uttered by Seamus was something new. An explosion of emotion gripped her.

"I can take care of you forever. Well, after this whole deal wraps up, anyway." Seamus frantically described whatever boondoggle land stitch up made him think he'd struck it rich, or would, shortly. He was certain of it. Millie listened carefully, but it was no use. Too complicated. Besides, Happy Seamus was far too distracting to begin to understand byzantine real estate financial matters. Stunned at optimism from the morose brooding boy she used to know, Millie saw out of the corner of her eye Papa go outside for a spell with Mr. Shearn, and seized the moment. Such a rare moment, when Seamus was accessible, present, joyful; but not yet drunk. She threw herself into his arms for their first kiss, their lips colliding years of unexpected desire, clumsy teenaged fireworks blasting in all directions, then softly melting into each other, a universe painting itself on a brand new canvas before their closed eyes. It was over before Papa returned inside, but Papa could tell something was up. Millie could hide nothing from Papa.

Giddy beyond words, Millie's performance that night soared; the first night she didn't see Seamus start a brawl, smiling to each other through the music.

4 RASSELAS MOWRY

A clock ticks in Rhode Island

Rhode Island was so filled with Mowrys by 1848, anyone without the name had all sorts of other names for them. Silver spoon, blue blood, silk stockings, patrician, aristocrat, "the landed"; little Rasselas Mowry had heard them all.

The family homestead in Smithfield teemed with Mowry children constantly. When the kids weren't helping farm the plot, racing around chasing each other, or in school, Rasselas' father Ziba and mother Everline gathered them 'round to tell the tales of the colonial patriarch, Nathaniel, arriving on this spot in any number of legendary ways in 1660 something. The tales varied based on who told them.

Mama's version had Nathaniel's father getting exiled into the wilderness from Plymouth colony for being some sort of heretic. Papa's version featured Nathaniel's father's arrival on the English ship *Blessing* in 1635, after which Nathaniel entered the world in 1644, somehow. Aunt Esther's story, which she never failed to tell on Christmas Eve from a rocking chair, was the best one. Rasselas and his four brothers gathered, Aunt Ester spun such a yarn about Nathaniel he seemed god like, hacking his family's birthright from the wilderness with his bare hands. The second youngest, by 7 years old in 1848, Rasselas had already had enough.

It was Sunday school that turned the worm. One Sunday, some holy man declared to the assembled children that by saying a certain prayer, in precisely the same way, at a certain time of day, some certain percentage of the Holy Spirit's miraculous power would accrue unto the devoted. So Rasselas, being good with math, and a kid, started adding it all up, figuring after saying this prayer correctly for a while, he could perform any miracle he chose. After five Sundays of saying this particular prayer at the perfect time in the perfect way, Rasselas calculated it was time to bend a spoon on the table by directing the Holy Spirit's power at it, with his stare.

The spoon didn't bend, of course. That summer day, Rasselas decided everyone in the Mowry family was a liar and a fraud. Over autumn, the family began to notice

Rasselas brood, shorter to anger, descending into books, and especially maps. When Aunt Esther told her colonial tales Christmas Eve, 1848, Rasselas sat at the base of the Christmas tree staring at a map of the frontier beyond the Mississippi River. Calling the children one by one to her lap, Aunt Esther rocked them along, as usual, "And what do all the Mowry children want for Christmas this year?" At his turn, Rasselas pointed a finger onto his map, randomly landing onto the word "Minnesota".

Rasselas was the only soul of 200 years of Mowrys in Smithfield with that given name. He hated it. By summer, 1849, at 8 years old, while Peter Marks choked on cotton dust in Liverpool, and Millie learned to play violin in St. Paul, he'd come to prefer Rassel. Rassel's father, Ziba, was only the second Mowry with his name, after his own father, Ziba Sr. Thus, father, son, and grandpa were close. When, like himself, Everline and Ziba's boy Rassel started to appear good with math, the father and son connection hardened like the masonry Ziba was known for.

Miles of stone wall in Smithfield owed their perfection to Rassel's dad, Ziba Mowry, Jr.. To help supplement the farm, Ziba learned carpentry from Harris Steere, another farmer on a family plot, just down the road in Smithfield. From carpentry, Ziba turned to building stone walls, such that not a road in Smithfield was missing a Ziba Mowry wall after a while, all the way south into Greenville, where Rasselas and his brothers went to school.

As soon as Rassel's hands were big enough to handle stones, Ziba took his son with him on the job as soon as school let out for summer. Left to work on the family farm, Rassel's four brothers were, of course, jealous. Crawford, the oldest at 13, never liked math or stones or carpentry, so he wasn't too bothered. Simon, 12, and Gilbert, 10, found adventure in the fields, but 3-year-old Albert took it personally, as toddlers do. Every time Rassel headed out with Papa, Albert raised a ruckus. Albert was spoiled, largely since both of Everline's daughters before him died early; Josephine at 11 months, Mary at 5 months. In 1849, Albert was the baby, molded into the most delicate of the Mowry children. Rassel's favorite moment leaving every morning to build walls with Papa that summer was when they rounded the first bend from home to make it out of earshot of Albert's morning tantrums.

Since Rassel figured out the year before that the power of the Holy Spirit wouldn't bend spoons for him, no matter how much of it he accumulated with magic words whispered in just that certain way, this summer he presented the sudden, skeptical curiosity of an eight-year-old, subjecting his father to an interrogation every single day. Cutting in some mortar between stones one afternoon, Ziba's frustration at being on Rassel's witness stand got the best of him.

"Why are there so many cotton mills around

Smithfield?" Rassel asked as Papa trowelled in the mortar.

"Water power." Ziba's answers to Rassel's endless questions were clipped quite short by late summer. Rassel positioned another stone, then another query.

"But why cotton?" Rassel insisted.

"It's cheap."

"Why is cotton cheap?" Ziba's mortaring accelerated.

"You should be happy it's cheap." Ziba pressed harder and harder into the mortar, something in him becoming hot, Rassel's summer long interrogation prying too close.

"But we don't make cheap stone walls!" Rassel went for another stone.

"Someday you may own one of those mills."

"Why would I want to make something cheap?" Rassel wondered.

"To feed your children," Ziba started to snap. The trowel pressed the mortar in a frenzy.

Rassel placed another stone. "Where do they get the cotton for all those mills?" Suddenly, Ziba pressed too hard on the mortar, and the stone fell off the wall onto his foot.

"DAMMIT!" Ziba hopped around in pain. Rassel rushed to his father's foot, crying with apologies. Ziba's limp on the way home eased until he'd walked it off, comforting Rassel who thought it was all his fault, for asking too many questions.

Widow Tucker's witches

Living next door to the Mowrys, Widow Tucker was only heard of. A rumor, a scandal ignored, a forgotten spinster to be isolated. People would take care of Widow Tucker here and there. Rassel's mom always sent him over with a pie or cake at Christmas. Papa would help with odd jobs. But in autumn 1849, the chill grey wind dangling tree limbs like bony fingers from the sky, terror struck the Mowry kids' hearts at the mere mention of the widow next door.

They'd rush across Widow Tucker's yard on scamps through the woods between the Mowry homestead and her creaky house. She was never seen; one glimpse of the house, and the boys ran for their lives. Around the hearth each night, they spun tales of close calls, of wickedness harbored by Widow Tucker waiting to seize little children but for their clever quickness at escape.

One dusk that October, Rassel's older brothers

Crawford, Simon, and Gilbert, raced past him on the way home through Widow Tucker's front yard so quickly they didn't hear 8 year old Rassel trip on a tree root, roll to the ground, and freeze there in a pile of leaves underneath which flies had gathered upon...something dead. Alone, Rassel stared up at the porch as the silhouette of the witchy woman appeared in her front window, still. She'd seen him. Rassel just knew it.

The flies made their presence known in a cloud over Rassel. He tried to sink deeper into the leaf pile, become one with the ground, to vanish away from the flies and Widow Tucker's gaze, both closing in. Moments lingered, Rassel trapped between discovery and a host of insects. Footsteps brushed through leaves toward the house, right past him. His every hesitant inhale captured a mouth or nose full of flies, so Rassel tried to stop breathing.

The footsteps came from three ladies in black who seemed to float up the porch steps. Widow Tucker disappeared from the window. The door whined open. Flies in his ears now, through their buzz Rassel heard each lady repeat the same thing to Widow Tucker as they entered, like a password, then the door closed. An oil lamp lit up the interior.

Bounding to his feet, Rassel flew home so fast he barely touched the ground, waving flies off of him, hurling into leaf piles to roll on the ground to cleanse of them. Bolting past the Mowry house to the well, Rassel pumped water over himself frantically. His stunned brothers ran to the well, surrounding their soaked, shivering little brother, who just stared forward, panting on the ground like a dog.

"She has witches," Rassel whispered, heaving for breath. "They cast a spell of flies!" Mama warmed Rassel up with a bath, then the boys spent another dark cold night around the hearth telling witchy tales until bedtime. Rassel couldn't fall asleep, horrified that Mama would send him to that house again with a Christmas pie, until chirping birds of the nearing dawn finally sang him off into dreams.

News that Widow Tucker had cast a spell of flies upon him took hold of Rassel's school in Greenville in no time, as kids did what kids do. By the end of November, 1849, 8 year old Rassel's part in the story had disappeared, Widow Tucker's wicked legend reaching heights only kids could conjure, so evil and other worldly, Rassel's skeptical nature kicked in. Like learning the Holy Spirit's power would not, actually, empower him to bend spoons with his mind, Rassel soon figured out Widow Tucker was no witch. Turned out everyone hated Widow Tucker, who none of them had met, guilt eating at Rassel for his part in making things worse.

Quietly, Rassel started listening very closely to every yarn spun about Widow Tucker - for clues. There must be some reason everyone was afraid of her. Not some witchy reason, no, a real reason, Rassel was sure of it. But it was useless. Every time Rassel thought he'd whacked past the thicket of ghoulish legend to something real, all he encountered was...silence. But those three ladies! The ones who walked right by Rassel as he lay on the ground swarmed by flies in front of Widow Tucker's house! Rassel's investigation turned up nothing on them, either. No one knew a thing, nor wanted to. It seemed the spell was cast not *by* Widow Tucker, but *at* her. A spell of silence.

For the first time, Rassel looked forward to delivering the pie Mama would bake for Widow Tucker every Christmas. He simply had to meet this witch and see for himself. As Mama was baking the usual bread one Saturday morning late in November, Rassel asked which sort of pie would go to Widow Tucker that Christmas. Papa overheard. A clue emerged, in the tone of Papa's voice, the same tone Papa used when Rassel asked about cotton mills that summer.

"Stop sending that woman pies!" Papa yelled.

"You'll do well to mind your own business," Mama snapped as she kneaded. That night, Rassel's mind raced as he tried to sleep, imagining what answers to his questions might await him behind Widow Tucker's exile of silence, soon to be unlocked by a Christmas pie.

Widow Tucker goes through her things

"I'm sorry we brought no Christmas pie, it's all my fault for making everyone think you're a witch," Little Rassel implored at Widow Tucker's front door one late January afternoon, so nervous and ashamed he trembled in the winter cold.

"Oh, people think I'm all sorts of things," Widow Tucker chuckled. "Do come in and warm up, young man!"

When Christmas came and went in 1849 without Mama sending Rassel next door with the annual Christmas pie for Widow Tucker, his kid instinct to question kicked into high gear. Rassel sensed the same silence shroud Widow Tucker's existence as when he asked Papa about cotton mills. Finally, on the walk home from school one day, Rassel summoned his courage, walked past the spot in her front yard where he'd fallen last autumn under the assumed witchy spell of flies, marched up Widow Tucker's porch stairs, and knocked, introducing himself as the boy next door.

"Now, what sort of witch was I, Mr. Mowry?" Widow Tucker teased, waddling toward her kitchen to make some hot milk.

"You cast a spell of flies on me," Rassel confessed, relieved that humor would govern his visit.

Widow Tucker burst into uproarious laughter, so persistent, Rasselas almost cried. "I'm so sorry, Mrs. Tucker!"

"My secret powers get better in old age!" Widow Tucker joked. "Do sit down."

"But who were those ladies?" Rassel wondered.

"Oh, just old friends from Pawtucket," Widow Tucker replied. "Very old friends."

A short visit at the hearth later, hot milk downed at kid speed, Widow Tucker waved goodbye from her porch. Rassel skipped home through the snow, forgiven for his childhood ways, with a new friend. Curiosity now insatiable, Rassel kept all he learned next door to himself, sleeping so soundly that night he had to be dragged out of bed for school the next morning. He rushed into the tiny schoolhouse, heading straight for his teacher, knowing his new quest must be kept out of earshot of anyone at home, an instinct the teacher's shocked response to his question confirmed.

"What happened in Pawtucket?" Rassel demanded. The teacher gasped, then changed the subject. Rassel was on his own again.

As the 1850 Rhode Island winter dragged on so long spring seemed nothing but a wish, Widow Tucker expected the April rains would bring back the curious and thoughtful little boy next door, eventually. It came as no shock that all the children in Smithfield thought her a witch. The surprise was that one of them, living next door, would pierce through all that somehow. So, after her short visit from Rasselas, Widow Tucker began to prepare for his return, digging back a quarter century, to her final days in Pawtucket in summer, 1824, when she became a widow.

Age was now a barrier. Widow Tucker hadn't thought of that box in a long time, where she kept hidden away all trace of the love of her life, in the tiny house's attic she hadn't climbed up to in years. Rickety old knees struggled onto each rung of the stepladder. Reaching into the loft was an exercise in hope, groping around in the dark to identify that box by feel. Dust fell onto her as she dragged it down the ladder, slowly, carefully. The dirty box on the floor, she sat back into the rocking chair before it, and sighed. Pausing to remember their love, she pried open the box, and on top inside, was a banner she tenderly unfurled for the first time in 26 years. "Down with the Lords of Lash and Loom!" screamed out from the mists of time once more, and Widow Tucker smiled, casting her mind back.

Slater Mill in Pawtucket in May, 1824, teemed with little children and young women loading slave harvested cotton into the looms. Business boomed as every mill in Rhode Island bustled to spin "negro cloth" to sell back to Southern plantation owners the clothes their slaves wore, made from the cotton they picked, capital's sick inexorable logic folding upon itself like a snake eating its own tail. Power looms had become too big for the children over the years, so by 1824, desperately poor young women like the newly wed Mrs. Tucker joined the children in the mill at a wage so meager her new husband had to grow carrots in their plot, tend chickens, even collect dandelion greens just to feed his new bride.

The May day the mill announced yet another a pay cut and yet longer hours, the young Mrs. Tucker's co-workers would not abide. They'd had enough. When Mrs. Tucker returned home from the mill to tell her husband the women called a "turnout", and why, Mr. Tucker beamed with pride, that night creating the banner for his wife to march with, scrawling her anger onto the negro cloth that stoked it. Across Pawtucket the women marched for weeks, the turnout spread across Rhode Island, strikers attacking mill owners' homes, owners fighting back, until a mill was burned to the ground. A compromise was somehow forged after the fire, and the mills reopened. Mr. and Mrs. Tucker were suddenly heroes in Pawtucket. The mill owners resolved none of it would ever happen again.

Her husband's body was found covered in flies on a roadside one morning that summer, just one message of retribution meted out with targeted, relentless, permanent precision across Rhode Island. There would be no more textile strikes. Mrs., now Widow Tucker, blacklisted into total poverty, that December gave birth to his child, who died within hours, because her mother had been starving for months by then. She was now viewed as cursed in Pawtucket, ostracized. Somehow, she managed to land in the dilapidated house on the Mowry homestead in Smithfield, far enough away from Pawtucket that her status as a childless widow would yield just enough pity, with no questions asked. The Pawtucket Textile Strike faded behind her, settling into years spent scraping sustenance from her charity granted plot, nights spent rocking in that chair to rest. Each passing year, she hoped ever more fervently it would be her last, as quiet exile engulfed her, and children conjured her into a witch.

Now, suddenly, she wanted to live again. After all, a curious little boy would soon visit, she was sure of it. And he needed to know. So the box was emptied, her husband resurrected, the memories displayed lovingly on every corner of her house, the banner unfurled again. Life returning to her soul, Widow Tucker's winter bed felt more cozy than usual that night under an extra quilt. Sinking into her pillow, for the first time in years, she forgot to beg the Lord to take her before waking up.

Rassel's struggle with peaches

Over the 200 or so years that generations of

Mowrys lived on their little homestead in Smithfield, fruit trees had become the prized produce of the plot. By the time Rasselas and his four brothers arrived, the trees were so old, copious, and fertile a carpet of fruit dropped from them every year for the kids to pick up off the ground. With peaches in summer, the work began by the end of June, then a break in late summer and early autumn, before the apples and pears fell. The youngest, Alfred, being hopelessly spoiled by age 4, was the first Mowry in two centuries to fail to carry on the tradition. Crawford, Simon and Gilbert before him decided this was the chore they hated most about farming, but Rasselas delighted in carefully sorting through the fruit on the acres of family land. His older brothers discarded far too many, grown indifferent by the numbing tedium and aching bending over. Rassel rarely tossed away any of the fruit. He did the math one day, figuring he saved at least five jars of jam more than his brothers did, every year. Mama would confirm, always more jam and apple butter work from Rassel's baskets.

Rassel's favorite was peaches; nothing like a summer peach. The Mowry peach trees produced spectacular specimens, each perfectly yellow, then orange, then a bit red under the most lovely peach fuzz when they were ready to pick. Spring blossoms made the orchard a glorious cathedral under which little Rassel grew up spending hours just gawking at them, the bees buzzing above him. As they ripened, Rassel would go for walks under the trees all spring, inspecting the metamorphosis from green to yellow, watching them grow, squeezing them a bit, waiting. He loved seeing the limbs bend under their growing weight, transforming the orchard into a series of umbrella canopies, until the first of them dropped to the ground; time to harvest. One of his happiest days of the year was when Rassel grabbed the stacks of baskets and headed to the orchard to get those perfect peaches before the best ones fell off the trees. The baskets in the barn were some of the oldest Mowry artifacts of the family. It was said the patriarch Nathaniel himself weaved a couple of these peach baskets in 1680 something.

Mama appointed Rassel Chief Peach Taster. As a toddler, he gorged himself sick with them such that Rassel's taste buds knew a good peach from a substandard one. The best ones immediately went into pies, turnovers, and all manner of summer bakery. The next category was set aside for canning. After that came the jam peaches, The final, not quite ripe category, were put outside to ripen in the sun for canning and jam. Peaches that were a bit wormy, or too ripe, went into the compost pile. By 1850's peach crop, at 10 years old Rassel was dying to learn the next logical step in his peach worship; making the pies. Mama always knew at some point she'd have to teach one of the boys to bake. Both her daughters gone as babies, passing down the traditions of cooking required careful attention to her boys, to learn which would bother with learning the old ways, the "woman's work", then passing it down themselves. For baking pies, she knew early on it would be Rassel, thus Mama graduated Rassel from field hand to taster to apprentice pastry chef in Mama's kitchen.

The battle commenced. In no time at all, Rassel learned it is one thing to harvest and devour peaches to the point of being a professional family taster, quite another to bake a pie out of them. Baking pastry seemed to come so easily to Mama. Her pie crusts were so flaky, just the right amount of salt and sugar balance, they baked up so golden brown, the bottom crust just soggy enough, the edges fluted exactly correct, the filling's stacks of sliced peaches arranged with total precision, yielding a slice of pie on a plate presenting pure art to the dessert portion. Every single point in this process, Rassel screwed up. He rolled the dough out too thick. Then he rolled it too thin, so it would break under the rolling pin. He tossed too much flour on the rolling pin, so the resulting crust hours later tasted like...flour. His fluted edges looked like an animal had wandered across his pie, leaving claw prints. A never ending series of pastry faux pas tormented Rassel for a week that summer of 1850 under Mama's watchful eye.

But the worst was his pie filling. The very nature of a peach pie, the peaches themselves, Rassel seemed to ruin, every single time. First, he chopped the peaches too thick, so they piled up into not a pie but a small mountain, thus when sliced the pie just fell apart on the plate. This also left a bath of peach juice at the bottom of the pie, like an ocean, destroying the bottom crust into a sort of goo. Little Alfred loved those pie failures, as Mama would give him the peach juice to drink. Then, Rassel sliced the peaches too thin, resulting in not so much a pie as a door stop, the oven hardening it to a mass of gelatinous...something. Too much sugar, or butter, left more peach juice bath. Not enough sugar left the peaches too hard. From one disaster to another, Rassel vacillated back and forth for a solid week. A succession of Rassel's failures got the entire family sick of eating his experiments, except little Alfred, who loved the peach pie juice.

"They're alright," Mama consoled after a week. "Baking is very difficult, Rasselas."

"I'm ruining it," Rasselas whimpered.

"It just takes practice. When I started making pies they all looked like yours."

"I wanted to bake the pie for Widow Tucker this Christmas and now look at this mess," Rassel complained. The mention of Widow Tucker startled Mama into changing the entire subject completely.

"How about I teach you to make the jam instead?"

"That sounds much easier," Rassel smiled, finally moving on from bakery.

A strange sort of funeral in Smithfield

Rasselas did not return to Widow Tucker's house until the day ten years later he came to empty her home after she died. By 1860, the town had surrounded little Rassel's interest in Widow Tucker the way white blood cells identify a viral threat, swarming the boy for ten years until he was a young man, with a fog of total silence. Everywhere little Rassel turned to learn about what happened to Widow Tucker in Pawtucket morphed into a brick wall. Fear gripped the boy such that Widow Tucker's home was now more terrifying than when he thought she was a witch. The silent swarm even changed the Mowry Christmas; no more pies sent next door. Rassel didn't dare go back.

As Rassel grew up on the Mowry farm, distance calcified between him and the rest of the Mowry family, especially his father, Ziba Jr., the fossilized throwback most determined to keep Rassel away from that witch. Withdrawn, quiet, bookish, Rasselas kept to himself, excelling at math, with hopes to be an engineer designing roads like those he'd built stonewalls along with his father. Rassel's interest in Widow Tucker's story faded so far back into his mind, the house next door was nearly invisible on his walks to school. Once in a while he resumed his quest, especially when he was old enough to go to the local taverns in Greenville, where scuttlebutt could be had once everyone was liquored up enough. There, he learned a bit about the Pawtucket Textile Strike; the safe late night drunken version only whispered across empty whiskey bottles. Shame gripped Rasselas for failing to visit Widow Tucker, so he'd get drunker, then his morning hangover would settle the exile instinct back onto his soul. Exile has a way of enforcing itself, through nameless fright.

No one even knew she'd died until another generation of kids thinking her a witch caught a whiff of whatever was rotting inside. The local undertaker never worked faster in his life, leaving the windows open so whatever was in there could get out before anyone else came in. One day that summer of 1860, Rassel's mother quietly suggested he go clean the house out for a new tenant. "I'll send your father to help," she said, never looking Rassel in the eye. Rassel knew what that meant, so finally returned to Widow Tucker's house, quickly, in order to beat his father there.

"Down With The Lords of Lash and Loom!" was the first thing he saw opening the front door, the 36 year old banner hanging where Widow Tucker had pinned it ten years ago, cobwebs dangling off it. Still exuding the faint hovering stench of death, all around the tiny house were the contents of her secret little box of memories. Papers, mementos, bits of negro cloth, a notebook, all more haunting than any witch Rassel had ever conjured her into as a child. Then there was the doll. Rassel stepped toward a hand sewn little bear, nestled into the corner of a chair, with a note lovingly pinned to it. He picked it up, hands trembling, to read the note. "Sewn from negro cloth for my daughter who passed away at birth." Rassel then knew; she had created a museum while waiting for him to return all these years, to tell the little boy next door her story. Frozen in disgust with himself, Rassel broke down in tears, surveying the room of documents and holy relics left to him, and him alone, when he was a child.

Papa marched in, determined, his eyes hawkish, like evil. It happened in the blink of Rassel's tears; stepping right past his weeping son holding a teddy bear, Papa ripped the banner from the wall, and Rassel ended his relationship with his father with one punch. A roundhouse right hook flew so fast from Rassel's torment it knocked his father flat, crashing him through a table, Widow Tucker's memories flying in all directions. Rasselas straddled across his prostrate father lying on his back, to stare down at Papa's loose tooth and the blood filling his throat, Rassel's glare daring him to get up. Get up you fucking coward. Thus Ziba Mowry, Jr., on his back from the floor, watched his son leave him forever, towering over him motionless, breathing heavy, a teddy bear clutched in his left hand, a fist still in his right, the wrath of history in his dead tearful eyes.

"You will clean...this house...yourself," Rassel said

softly, then stepped over his father on the floor, tossing the teddy bear back at him through the open front door. In the short walk home, Rasselas Mowry resolved that moment to get the hell out of Rhode Island forever, as fast as he could. By next summer, he would be in St. Paul, enlisted in Company A of the First Minnesota Volunteer Infantry.

5 THE SWAN

The Ghost dreams Peter to America

One evening, on Peter's regular sneak into Paul's room in servants' chambers at Arley Hall, he told Paul everything; the revolution, the march across Europe in rags, his childhood in Prussia, even how Bipkins snuck him into Arley Hall from the refugee trail. Paul was astonished, and more in love with Peter than ever.

"You have to know," Peter said, before a kiss began their night together. Afterward, exhausted in each other's arms, both knew there were big decisions ahead, but all they could do was hold each other closer than they'd done before, until sleep came, when The First Ghost of Gettysburg blew into Peter's dreams, to dance.

The Ghost summoned into Peter's sleep a red sky choked with smoke. There were yells, of thousands of men, screechy yelps of fury. A field of wheat. A creek bed. Rocks. Then, silence, the red sky became blue, the wheat field turned to raging seas, and Peter sat in a row boat, alone. As an eagle, the Ghost soared above, squawking the yells that had come from the men across the field that was now gone. Suddenly silence. The sea heaved towering waves, for what seemed eternity. Up. Down. No end.

The sea turned red, then narrowed, instantly into...a creek bed, Peter's boat too big for it, lodging into the stones. He was stuck. Peter stood in the boat. Silence. Motionless. Forever.

He stared toward the distant sky which was back to red. The creek opened to an ocean again, the boat floated onward, Peter standing in it, swept forward at incredible pace, surfing the heaving waves, up to the crest, then down. Another eternity began, at sea.

The sky now to blue from red, the wheat field appeared at the horizon and grew, approaching. Peter's tiny boat rushed ashore from the top of a wave into the flowing grain, skidding to a stop near a cabin. Calm overcame him, deep peace, so he rested, falling into the flowing grain, sleep returning from torment. But the Ghost was not finished.

Peter looked up at the cabin. A breeze blew up.

The door opened, and Paul walked out in his footman tuxedo, expressionless. A trickle of red flowed slowly from the cabin between Paul's feet toward Peter on the ground in the grain, burgeoning to a flood. The creek bed again. The rocks returned. The sky filled black with smoke again. The shrieks and yells roared up again, the trickle now a deep raging river of blood coming for Peter. He grasped for strands of grain, at the rocks, but they were gone.

The Ghost danced before Peter as he groped hopelessly for anything to hang onto. It was there, and not, the dance; a torment upon Peter, not even a mirage, just a thought; a realization that something frolicked to mock him as he lost balance. A void opened below Peter.

He began to fall.

"Peter!" someone cried out. He opened his eyes, gasping for air, waving to grab something anything, grabbing only Paul. "Wake up!"

It was over. Back in Paul's bed at Arley Hall, Paul leaned across the pillow over Peter and shook him. "It's me! Wake up! What a dream!"

"You're...you're here..."

"Indeed I am, and you're here, too, it's alright..."

Peter breathed normally again, finding his bearings, sitting up in bed.

"We have to get out of here, Paul."

"It's ok, it's just my room..."

"No, no, we have to leave Arley Hall. This is all no good! I'm so sorry..."

"Sorry for what?" Paul became confused.

"For all...for all this."

Paul insisted, "Well, I'm not!"

They paused, Peter put his head in his hands, rubbing through his hair.

"You were in my dream just now."

"I should hope so!"

Peter sighed. "I'm so sorry I got you into ... whatever my life is."

"If we have to leave, we go together," Paul declared, determined. "What about that hedge clipping chap who brought you to Arley Hall? Maybe he can help us out somehow."

Peter paused, curiously. "Bipkins?"

"He got you in here, maybe he can get us both out, together?"

They laid back down to try to get back to sleep.

Paul stared into Peter's eyes, to calm him, and tell him he loved him. As they began to nod off, Peter pulled the covers up.

"Yes, Bipkins," Peter whispered. The Ghost's work done, it left them both to sleep. Their next night off a week later, Paul followed Peter like a puppy to the George & Dragon, the village pub on the Arley Hall estate in Great Budworth. Certain Bipkins would be there, Peter charged in, ordered a round, and they waited. And waited, while they drank, and drank.

Soon, Paul had cast caution out the pub window, as Peter's German liver's tolerance kept watch over Paul's first good drunk. Peter hadn't been so happy since the early days of the revolution in Prussia, the heady days, of victory and change. They cared little who saw what, so free, the entire pub was infected with their joy, dance, song, and laughter.

"Where is this Bipkins of which you speak?" Paul joked as they fell into a corner, night deepening, revelry all around.

"He'll be here," and with that, there Bipkins was. Peter leapt to his feet with a bawdy German welcome. "Bipkins, old boy!"

"Seems I'm a drink behind!" Bipkins laughed, hurrying to catch up, pint after pint, amazing Paul. Peter kept himself together, only just. There was business to discuss, and Bipkins knew it. Huddled in the dark corner, business began.

"Now Bipkins," Peter leaned in, a bit wobbly, "You must know, that I know..." thoughts wandering, "that you know, that I KNOW, that..." Peter belched. Steadiness was elusive.

"That you're a German revolutionary on the run," Bipkins winked. Peter slammed the table.

"HOW? How... on earth...did you know that?" Peter summoned his German liver by ordering another round with a wave to the bar. The moment demanded focus, but also beer.

"You're not the first ragged refugee to wander through this village, old boy." As another round arrived at the table, Bipkins began to realize Paul wasn't just Peter's new friend. Something was afoot. They smiled at each other too...much. "I see you've made a friend at Arley Hall, you have!" Bipkins declared.

Paul giggled without care, "More than friends, old chap."

Bipkins leaned back, sighed, and understood. "It's always a revolution with you boys, isn't it?"

"You see, Bipkins, we love each other," Peter announced. "It's a bit of a pickle."

"Mr. Marks," Bipkins declared, raising his pint to

down it in one go, "I knew you'd make this all verrrry complicated!"

"You're the one who put me into Arley Hall!"

"Looked like you needed a room, you did!" Bipkins smiled wryly. "I didn't think you'd...well...fall in love with a footman?!"

"Then you are quite aware of our..." Peter motioned between himself and Paul, "...predicament."

Bipkins turned serious. "Must say this is a new one..."

"Two footmen in love!" Paul saluted. "At your service good sir!"

They'd disarmed Bipkins, or the beer had. Bipkins returned salute. "You've got a comrade in old Bipkins, you have!"

"Now," Peter began, swaying, but steadying, mightily, "We both need to leave Arley Hall."

"You know it will be very difficult for you," Bipkins warned. "Arley Hall is quite comfortable."

"Quite indeed," Peter agreed.

"But where I can send you is another world entirely," Bipkins continued. "I'm sure you've marched halfway across Europe, Mr. Marks, finding shelter wherever you might, but the boy here will find things most difficult. And that's if I can even do *anything* for you!"

"You do understand our problem, don't you Bipkins?" Peter pushed. "If I'm found out, or..." Peter waved between himself and Paul again, "...or any of this, it won't matter how comfortable Arley Hall was before that, now will it?"

Bipkins paused, staring at the table in disbelief and confusion. Paul, beer courage having seized him, sensed the moment, thus Paul's first good drunk suddenly gave way to the first time he'd ever stood up for himself, if with awkward timing. "Missssster Bipkins," Paul asked, catching his bearings, "if you cannot help us, well...who needs you?"

Peter tried to calm him. "Now, hold on..."

Paul had none of it. "I must say, my dear Bipkins, we leave Arley Hall together, Peter and I, and it matters to me not one whit *to where*, or *to whom*, or how uncomfortable. You think I'm incapable of suffering? I can show you my good fellow! If you cannot help us in this regard, good sir..."

"That's enough, Paul," Peter interrupted, which Paul ignored, leaning toward Bipkins, whose apprehension was now surprise at Paul's insistence.

"I do appreciate your help Mr. Bipkins, but if it is

not of the sort that keeps me with Peter, than I do not want it." Peter's Germanness ballooned with pride at Paul's sudden bravery, while his revolutionary instincts shuddered at Paul's indiscretion.

"Let's not make a scene, Paul," Peter insisted, suppressing laughter at Paul's performance, lest it encourage him.

"We will stay together, Peter, or...," the beer momentarily halted Paul, then he recovered, "...or we die alone!" Paul then realized he'd overdone it, becoming embarrassed slightly. "Anyway, Mr. Bipkins, I'm sure you understand." He sat down, finally, to everyone's relief.

"You see, Bipkins, this is quite serious indeed!" Peter chuckled.

Bipkins thought one last moment, and decided. "You'll need a cover story."

Paul celebrated. "Now, that's the spirit old boy!"

"You'll have to be 'brothers', you see," Bipkins announced.

Paul perked up brightly, raising his pint, then downing it, declaring, "Brothers in arms!" Peter's German laugh erupted, Bipkins smiled and shook their hands as if they'd closed a real estate deal. All business.

"This calls for another round," Peter demanded.

"I will get those pints, I will," Bipkins declared standing up, "and you have my word, gentlemen, that if you both cannot be welcomed where I can send you, I will not send you there." Peter and Paul watched Bipkins push through the crowded pub toward the bar, then turned to each other with disbelief and wonder.

Beaming with pride at the deal he'd just closed, Paul gushed, "This is quite a fine start, isn't it?"

Bipkins takes tea with Lizzie & Mary Burns

"They're '*brothers*', you say," Lizzie smirked at Bipkins as he entered the front door of a rather plain terrace in Manchester where Lizzie and her sister Mary kept house for a mysterious gentleman.

"Indeed, brothers they are!" Bipkins replied sheepishly.

"You know, Bipkins," Lizzie continued playfully in her Irish brogue, ushering Bipkins to the sitting room, "we've not lost our faculties." Lizzie cocked her head with a grin. Bipkins seated himself as they spoke in the familiar riddles of the underground. Layers of cover, each more deceptive than the one before, were as familiar to Lizzie and Mary Burns as their own hairpins. Bipkins didn't even know whose house he was in, and never would.

From the Irish slums of Manchester, the two young sisters Lizzie and Mary Burns somehow became as known to the revolutionary underground as Queen Victoria herself; unnamed lady shadows, just "the sisters". In a crisis, one turned to Lizzie or Mary, if one could find them. Bipkins could find them, at any moment. Nestled in the countryside midway between Liverpool's docks and the teeming smokestacks of Manchester, the villages around Arley Hall had become by 1850 a sort of weigh station on the revolutionary refugee trail. German foot soldiers like Peter Marks had been crisscrossing the whole of the UK since 1849 in this way, on the run. Lizzie and Mary were known to help them along, find them shelter, often even a job in one of Manchester's filthy cotton mills, where Lizzie and Mary had long ago steeply paid their dues. No one knew why Lizzie and Mary could pull rabbits out of hats like this, only that there existed a secret gentleman upon whom they relied to work their magic, and that the Burns sisters kept his house.

Bipkins fell enmeshed into such intrigues purely by chance of clipping the hedges on the Arley estate. Nothing but a tenant on Arley's vast holdings, he'd see the refugees wander the roads, like Peter Marks, and take pity. Being clever, it took Bipkins little time to navigate the webs all the way to Lizzie and Mary in Manchester, out of pure desperation to move refugees further inland, deeper into the byzantine obscurity of Britain's burgeoning industrial honeycomb, into the smoke and slums, to disappear. One thing led to another, always, until finding himself with two "brothers" to hide was merely another puzzle for Bipkins to solve.

"His Lordship thinks a footman from the cousins' Westphalia castle fled to Arley", Bipkins explained, crossing his legs.

Lizzie chuckled. "And this German footman has a brother?"

Mary entered with a tray of afternoon tea. "Ahhhh, Mary, lovely to see you, it is!"

"What trouble have you brought us now, Bipkins?" Mary asked, serving Bipkins his tea, taking a seat to set some ground rules. "Now Bipkins, my sister does not need another dashing young revolutionary to swoon over."

"Oh, Mary," Lizzie scolded, "From what Bipkins tells me this trouble shall swoon over neither me, nor you." Mary paused to stare at Bipkins. Bipkins shrugged.

"This one's for the books, Mary," Bipkins declared, sipping his tea. Mary looked to Lizzie with surprised realization. Lizzie shrugged too, grinning.

"Bipkins, you devil! Always outdoing yourself!" Mary laughed.

"Just a hedge clipper, I am, milady!" Over tea, it

was discussed then decided.

"I know just the molly house for them," announced Mary walking Bipkins to the door. He paused, turning at the door to ask a question he knew the answer to.

"Will you ever tell me whose house this is, Mary?"

"Never. And never shall you ask again."

A dark night a week later, Lizzie Burns opened the door to the flat above the molly house pub, The Swan, ushering in the last moment of Peter's fullness. There, The Ghost returned, oozing from the creaks of the door to envelope Peter in slow motion. A step across the transom, his foot hovering above it, then down, the floor beneath him bent loudly. A pause.

Two beds. A small desk. There's a window onto the street below the tiny, empty room. In the time it took to lift his back foot forward to step further into the room, Peter's mind raced backward, The Ghost waiting patiently for Peter to realize it had all gone wrong.

Seeing neither bed had been slept in, no bags, no clothes, Peter's second step into the room landed, groaning the floor board, its moaned cracking casting his eyes' gaze in reverse toward the firing synapses of his terrified mind, ablaze with regretful retracing of his every step from Arley Hall to this room that night. Confusion consumed him, his knees trembled into a blinded third step across the room to stand and stare, into himself.

There, The Ghost unleashed the screeches and yells of the nightmare in Paul's bed; the guns, the raging river and seas of blood, the smoke, the field. An eon passed as his hands reached to hold his head, bowed into his palms, fingers pressed into his temples to beg himself why. Why? Where? How? The Ghost silenced the wails as a rat scurried across the room, its feet scratching the wood floor, breaking the spell. The Ghost was gone. Peter stood in silence, sighing, looking this way then that at the cramped emptiness. He turned to face Lizzie, who stood in the doorway oblivious and business like.

"This is where you both can stay," Lizzie said, unaware of Peter's journey to a thousand worlds just then.

"Where is he?" Peter managed, barely a bleak desperation in his whisper.

"I don't know," Lizzie said. "I brought him here last night, wasn't that the plan?" The Plan, Peter thought. Ah, yes, plans. Another joke was on him, clarity quieting Peter's fogged mind. He laughed to himself.

"The plan," he chuckled grimly, and Lizzie finally saw Peter's sorrow, then understood. She stepped toward him into the room.

"Oh dear," she said softly, summoning the gallows humor of the underground, where plans go wrong by rule, leaving nothing but fatalistic futility behind. "'The Plan' it was, wasn't it," she said with a wry grin, mercy in her voice. Peter heaved a deep breath, looked at the ceiling, then down, to see, actually see, Lizzie. Beautiful and plain, like a young mother, Lizzie reached out to brush Peter's collar, to primp his ascot just so, the final reminder of Peter's days as a silly Prussian schoolboy, or a footman to the inbred patricians he'd just escaped. "Never mind the plan, Mr. Marks," she declared.

"I have to find him," Peter struggled through a smile. Lizzie didn't have the heart to tell Peter that a molly house in this nook of Manchester would instantaneously make a meal of an impossibly handsome, alone little fellow like Paul, leading him to places unknown pitilessly. She'd ushered Paul to this same room last night, knowing upon seeing him Paul would be the object of every thirsty upper class slum tourist who'd lay eyes on him, chum to a pool of sharks. She'd have been shocked if Paul were waiting there when she brought Peter in. Finding Peter equally easy on her eyes, Lizzie ignored her big sister Mary's cautions against swooning over dashing revolutionaries, as the moment required a bit of swooning. Thus, Lizzie began to care for Peter Marks.

"Mr. Egan is the proprietor of The Swan," she began, "and you are the new bartender here. It's a sort of gentlemen's club...for certain..."

"Gentlemen," Peter finished, coyly coming

around.

"Why, yes, and frankly, I'm one of the very few ladies who ever set foot in this place. Only the mollies come here, and I must warn you, they will find you most intriguing, indeed." Peter began to understand. "Egan does not expect you to work tonight, so just get some rest. You've had quite a day."

Rest, Peter laughed to himself. As soon as Lizzie was gone, Peter ran down the stairs into the dark smoky hive of "gentlemen" in various debauched states of lounging, carefully sneaking unseen to the bar to find Egan polishing some pint glasses, who expected him, and his desperation.

"The boy from last night?" Egan asked Peter.

"Where is he?" Peter implored.

Egan marks Peter's territory

Days passed to weeks as Peter settled into bartending at The Swan, thinking of Paul every moment. Mr. Egan quickly learned Peter was a revenue generator, a prized peak every patron sought to summit so fervently that word spread of the handsome forbidden fruit barkeep. Business thus boomed. Peter kept it all at arm's length, his only interest finding Paul, a miracle fading fast.

He made no friends, only regulars, whose favorites he committed to memory. So focused on work, Peter made The Swan the tidiest, best kept molly house in the whole of the Midlands. "Mollies", the pejorative term for gay men in Victorian England, had never had such a pleasant hideaway. Outside, The Swan looked as filthy, run-down wretched and forgotten as any dive pub in any slum. Inside, a Prussian gentleman doted on every detail as only a veteran footman of Arley Hall could. All Peter's upper class skills were directed at Mr. Egan's business with revolutionary military precision.

Running a molly house was never a family affair, and Egan never a family man. As things did in the Victorian gay underground, Egan's life plopped him into pubbing quite by chance. One toxic relationship led to another, a plot twist, then the slum and streets, then a pub he owned. What could he say? Middle age made him grateful just for steady income even if it was at the margins of society one step ahead of the law. Any day Egan's pub could be raided, everyone rounded up, and his life over. Such precarious circumstance crossed Egan's path with many in the underground, radical or not, gay or straight. To Lizzie and Mary Burns, The Swan was just one more safe zone, one more vector collected over years of struggle, if a bit more adventurous. Egan, like Bipkins at Arley Hall, was a resource to the Burns sisters, a harbor in a storm, a comrade, who could disappear tomorrow. Peter's arrival was just a bit more adventurous than the average underground occurrence.

Egan could barely believe his good fortune, so began to watch over Peter like a son. Like all the other mollies, Egan found Peter attractive beyond measure, which only served as a lesson. Being rather plump, ruffled, and homely, Egan once wished to possess Peter's looks himself. Upon seeing how those looks brought Peter nothing but constant leering, unwanted affections, and swarms of buzzing vultures, Egan learned otherwise, so spared Peter that sort of attention, instead becoming Peter's protector, on his second night in the upstairs flat. Before Lizzie Burns needed it for "two brothers," Egan had rented the upstairs room out per night, for various trysts. Egan thought it good business to trade the room's private love nest revenue for labor, which his patrons learned the hard way through a gentleman in frills, whose impertinence on Peter's second night at The Swan became quite the tattle in the gossipy air of molly England.

An upper class patron, drunk, dressed in ladies finery and whatnot, had spent all night pitching various woo at Peter the new boy, somehow learning he stayed upstairs. Egan watched this prince sneak up the stairs to wait for Peter's shift to end, gave him just enough time to get comfortable, then marched up behind him, leaving Peter oblivious at the bar to clean up for closing.

Egan burst into the room like a stalking lion to find the gentleman with corset available on Peter's bed prepared for his assumed romantic evening. Egan set upon him, locked him by his neck, held his pocket knife there, then squeezed the air out of his lungs with all his strength. "This room is closed for business," Egan whispered into the frilly gentleman's terrified ear, "and if I catch you or anyone else in here again you will have breathed your last." Then Egan dragged the toff to the stairs hurling him down in a heap. From behind the bar cleaning wine glasses, Peter caught just a glimpse of the princely petticoat cascading down. The gentleman popped off the floor to run out limping terribly, and Peter knew then he'd found a home. Egan waddled down the stairs wiping his forehead with a handkerchief, exhausted by the sudden exertion of manhood he hadn't had to deploy in years, sauntering up in a swagger and a smile to Peter, whose tidying up was now as vigorous and joyful as Arley Hall had ever required, or received.

"I'm getting too old for this, Mr. Marks," Egan sighed folding his hanky, now knowing what happened to Paul, determined it not happen to Peter. From that moment, Peter transformed The Swan into the crown jewel molly house of Her Majesty's realm. Work channeled and distracted Peter's deep torment about Paul. Where was he? What had happened? Every night, Peter carefully deployed the tactics of clandestine search he learned on the march during the revolution. Keep your eyes open, your ears more so, and your mouth shut. Egan noticed it all, volunteering his own efforts here and there, asking this patron or that a few things. Nothing ever came of it. Paul was gone.

Lizzie blows her cover for Peter

Peter lost track of time at The Swan. Might have been a year, maybe two, maybe more, until Lizzie Burns returned one hot summer afternoon when business was slow. Peter was alone inside, leaning against the back of the bar, reading a newspaper, smoking a cigar, as the door opened and Lizzie appeared, jarring Peter back to his dusty memories. He'd long ago forgotten Paul, that night he arrived from Arley Hall, the revolution, his previous three or four lives, everything. He was just a barkeep now, lucky to be working, and for a couple of years at that. But her eyes; those, Peter remembered, as Lizzie walked in with a smile, removed her hat, and saddled up to the bar.

"What took you so long?" Peter said, resigning himself to a trip down memory lane he'd rather not take, accepting that here was a challenge to endure with a potential prize at the end of it.

"Mr. Marks, you seem to have settled in very nicely," Lizzie said hopping onto a barstool. Peter turned on the charm.

"What can I get for you Miss Burns? It's Lizzie, yes?"

"You remember!"

"How could one forget?"

"You decide. I'll have whatever is prepared for the rare lady who comes in here." So it began. They circled each other's thoughts carefully. Every trick Peter kept hidden from The Swan's patrons he deployed onto Lizzie, sitting there, unable to avoid his spell. Halfway through the champagne from the perfectly polished long stem glass Peter presented, Lizzie tapped the bar with her fingers, nervous.

"Now, Mr. Marks," she began.

"I knew there'd be something," Peter smirked.

Lizzie paused to become serious. "Someone I know would like to help you."

"Oh?" Peter laughed, barely curious. "As you can see, Miss Burns, I don't need much help just now, but thank you. You've been help enough, I can't begin to express my gratitude."

"You don't understand," Lizzie insisted. By now, Peter's distrust of all around him was so thick, this was all just a little game to him.

"Do help me to understand," Peter replied, polishing pint glasses.

"Would you mind joining me for a walk?" Why

not, Peter thought. He locked the pub, following Lizzie through the teeming mid-summer Manchester slums, chatting nothingness the whole way, all just a prelude to Peter's first conquest since he fell in love with a footman who vanished. Lizzie made Peter feel alive again, engaged, interested. Her Irish brogue mixing with his Prussian accent seemed to all...fit; two comrades against the world, on a summer day. It was a fine little walk, until they turned a certain corner, Lizzie pointed to a doorway on a cotton mill, Peter saw the sign on the building, and rusted wheels in his mind began to pop, crank, then turn, backward.

"Ermen and who???" Peter gasped.

"Mr. Friedrich Engels," Lizzie said business like, "He'd like to meet you and offer you a position." Peter turned from the sign to look at Lizzie with such horror, Lizzie knew immediately she'd just stepped in it. "Now, Mr. Marks, please..."

"Why don't you leave me the HELL alone, Miss Burns!"

"Look here, Mr. Marks..."

"No you look here, Miss Burns, I've seen you twice in my life and each time you've blown it to pieces. Do you not know who this man is?"

"Of course I do, that's why I brought you here." Peter looked up at the cotton mill. Lizzie waited; she'd miscalculated terribly. Peter paced. He'd known this Engels in the revolution, on the retreating march into the mountains. All Peter's foot soldier comrades had come to despise Engels as nothing but a camp following intellectual pretender, a military novice of landed gentry lineage posing as a general to attach himself to actual generals thus festoon himself with the word "attaché", a kind of tourist collecting bona fides among the thousands who bled while he did no such thing, and never would. Whose father owned a bloody cotton mill. Now, here Peter was, staring at that mill, with a lady trying to usher him inside it; for a "position".

"Is he in there??"

"He's waiting for you."

"He knows me??"

"No, he knows a former comrade is in Manchester, that's all."

"What did you tell him??"

"Just that another comrade from his war days was in town...who is very talented."

"I want nothing from that man, Miss Burns. How on earth do you know him?"

"I...I keep his house with my sister." Peter's mind reeled as all the pieces fell together. Watching Peter melt down so unexpectedly, Lizzie realized she'd hurt him. All she wanted to do was help, and now, here was a catastrophe before her. "Mr. Marks, I'm so sorry, I just wanted..."

"You wanted to help, yes, I'm quite aware." Peter spit into the street in disgust. Why did he ever leave his parents in Prussia? Why did he ever leave Arley Hall? Why anything. "Miss Burns, you've been nothing but trouble to me!" Lizzie could feel Peter's heart breaking again, his mind lost, again. Such moments were common in the underground, so many roads dead-ending, twists, turns, false starts, broken hearts, all reaching at each other for comfort, against all odds, begging for connection amidst chaos.

"I can't...," Peter struggled, "I need to forget that world, Miss Burns, and the world after it. My world now is The Swan. I just want to be in one world, and stay in that world."

Lizzie gave up. "I'm very sorry, Mr. Marks, you'll never see me again," and turned to leave. Peter grabbed her arm.

"Oh no you don't," he said, spinning her toward him, locking her in his embrace. "Let's come to an arrangement, shall we?" Peter demanded.

"Mr. Marks...," Lizzie was suddenly disarmed. Their eyes met, locked into each other's agony, and hope.

"You stop trying to offer me help, and I'll enjoy

your company without it. Deal?" With an explosive kiss, thus began Peter's second love.

The King and Queen of The Swan

Peter and Lizzie's love affair had a "get while the getting's good" feel to it. They did not "court"; always just straight to it in the upstairs flat. They'd both been burned, all too common in their circles. There in bed, Peter learned how Lizzie and her sister Mary were guides for Engels into the Irish slums, so he could learn how the working class lived, then write about it while they toiled in his father's mill. Lizzie learned how Engels played a Little Napoleon in the revolution. They talked, and talked. Sharing their radical pasts so intimately was a refreshing oasis, but both were still wary of getting too close. Before opening the pub for that first evening, Peter made some coffee for Lizzie at the bar, as if it were just another day.

"You may be the first lady to ever be in that room," Peter teased.

"Twice, even," Lizzie reminded.

"When will I see you again?" Peter asked, ready for disappointment; trained by it.

"Tomorrow. My sister warned me about you." Stealing a night or afternoon in the upstairs flat would have to do for this love, lest scandalous questions be asked about the lady now a regular at a molly house. Once again, Peter's love was in hiding. No matter the effort, however, there was no hiding it from Egan.

After a month or two, Egan got used to Lizzie's visits, just rolling his eyes at the whole matter. He'd never seen a man go from loving another man to loving a woman so breezily, as Peter had gone from Paul to Lizzie. Egan took pride in it, reasoning it meant his was thus a molly house above all others in every respect. Peter's doting on the tiniest details of the pub accelerated as his affair with Lizzie grew longer, as if Peter was nesting. No gentleman's club compared, anywhere in the whole of England. Egan never had it so good.

But Egan worried. "Don't stand out" is the first rule of any underground enterprise, be it upstanding business or radical plot. The Swan was standing out, smack dab in the crossroads between the radical and upstanding. The clientele became more upper class, weekend crowds grew, the rumor of a mysterious lady lurking about only made the place more intoxicating to all. Word began to spread there was no better night out anywhere than at The Swan, for man or woman. What a pub! It all scared Egan terribly, even as the money rolled in. Molly houses existed constantly on the edge of obliteration; one careless word spreading just far enough, and the constabulary shut it down. Egan knew careless words were beginning to swarm The Swan, and not a thing he could do about it. He approached Peter.

"It would do for you to meet Lizzie elsewhere, you know," Egan warned one morning over breakfast.

"I wish I could, but I've no idea where she lives," Peter replied.

"I do. She thinks no one does, but in this business, one hears everything," Egan said. Soon, Peter was at the door of the unassuming terraced row house, unannounced. Mary Burns answered, horrified. Mary knew right away Lizzie had fallen for yet another dashing revolutionary, this one particularly fetching, and so clever as to find her home. She briefly swooned over Peter herself at the doorway, not letting him in, shooing him away. Lizzie arrived that night more nervous than usual, having been duly scolded by her older sister, arriving while Peter was at the market.

"You go easy on that fellow," Egan cautioned Lizzie, pouring her whiskey.

"You sound like my sister," Lizzie replied, tossing back the shot, then heading upstairs to wait.

"Irish girls," Egan shook his head. "Don't you chase him off, Miss Burns! That boy's the best thing that ever happened to The Swan."

Charging up the stairs, Lizzie declared, "Perhaps he loves me!"

Egan took a chug from the bottle of whisky, muttering to himself, "That's a lesson that boy will learn the hard way again."

The Ghost chases Peter to the docks

For weeks before The Swan was finally raided that night in summer 1856, impending dread enveloped Peter. Lizzie hadn't visited for a month. Egan noticed too, his disposition changing from jolly pub keeper to a tired, aging molly knowing his days were numbered. More popular than ever, The Swan's raucous crowds seemed a harbinger. Peter wondered what next, if this all ends? He'd taken to keeping a packed bag under his bed, just in case. But it can't end. Please, no, Peter begged the heavens. So weary of running, from one life to another, Peter otherwise lived in denial, refusing to believe the world he'd built for himself was just another short respite, clinging to its fantastical permanence, The Swan made near perfect by his own hard work, his own personality, perseverance, and protection. Here was a world he forged himself, for himself. Reality crashed into it.

Peter was luckily up in the flat. A regular had asked for the special aged scotch that had become Peter's trademark cocktail. So rare was this bottle, Egan had Peter keep it upstairs, lest it run out and be unavailable for the special customers who would drink nothing else. Another of Peter's personal flare he added to his world and all who entered it, that scotch was part of what made The Swan Peter's home. The knickknacks in his room, the way he stacked his books, hung his hat, fluffed his pillow, just...so. Ever since Lizzie returned and their love affair completed his tiny little life in a corner of Manchester's slums, Peter's nesting had become so thorough he'd notice a glass stacked wrongly, a mixing spoon out of place, his regulars being a tad late, or early. It was a life, a good one. Under the bed, as he reached for that precious scotch bottle nestled next to his packed haversack, it ended.

He heard Her Majesty's finest swoop in downstairs just as he gripped the bottle. By instinct, Peter scurried off the floor with the haversack, grabbed the cash box where he kept his wages, threw it in the bag, slinging it over his shoulder, leaving the bottle on the floor, like his life, again. At the top of the stairs, Peter waited for the throng of police to get far enough inside, then bolted down out the door behind them before they ran upstairs to satiate their well known degenerate bizarre interest in arresting mollies in the act, in bed. As paddy wagons rolled up to collect every molly inside and turn their lives to shambles, Peter glimpsed back inside, only to see Egan getting handcuffed by a bobby laughing hysterically at his power to destroy happy lives. Then, Peter sprinted off into the familiar chaos of his world yet again shattered like broken glass into tiny countless pieces, everywhere, and nowhere.

It was near midnight. Peter ran in a panic to the house Lizzie and Mary Burns kept for Engels in the terrace. Before knocking, he could tell they'd been gone for weeks. Sheets were in the windows, flowers in the front garden gone. Peter knocked anyway, desperately. Nothing. He cursed Engels for being such a coward he turned his love's life upside down just to run and hide while she kept his house. Typical. He probably made Lizzie and Mary pack his own bags. By 2am he stood panting outside Ermen and Engels' mill, screaming up at it, questioning every decision he'd ever made. Fate seemed determined to hurt Peter more the harder he worked, the better he made things around him, the more he loved. Still, Peter grasped for what remained, at the last hope that popped into his mind...Bipkins.

So Peter walked out of Manchester in the black of night, to the village lane where they met seven years ago. He was sure Bipkins would be trimming hedges at some point, just like before, so slept in the field near them. The Ghost returned in Peter's sleep, recasting the nightmare of heaving seas, screeches of a thousand men, until the sunrise woke Peter to wait for Bipkins until dusk. Just what Bipkins could do to help when Peter found him was something Peter didn't consider at all. All that mattered was that surely he'd be there at dusk, like last time.

All day Peter waited. He bought some fruit off a passing wagon to stave off hunger. Again at the mercy of

English weather, rain came and soaked Peter tented under his flimsy summer coat. The sky cleared. The sun set, but no Bipkins trimming hedges. Two and two finally came together in Peter's mind; they'd all gone back underground. Word got out, everyone scattered before it was too late. The Swan was too good to stay true, everything always was. Seven years in England, all now vanished, Peter laid back down in the field at the hedges, briefly considering returning to Arley Hall, as if nothing had happened. Idiocy, Peter decided; Arley Hall welcoming him back was less likely then being welcomed back into his father's Prussian aristocracy. He went back to sleep in forlorn hope that the next morning would return Bipkins to the hedges. Only The Ghost's nightmare returned.

Morning broke, then so did Peter. He cried like an infant on the soggy ground, covered in mud. Collecting himself, he knew what had to happen. No point avoiding it any longer. Time to run again. Leave. Get out. Unwashed for two days, Peter again reeked, smelling himself as he did the day he arrived at Arley Hall. It was all poetry, German tragedy; better even than the Greek sort, Peter thought. The cash box would be enough to get on the first ship he saw to his next life, it matters not where. Just...start all over again. He waited another futile morning hour for Bipkins. Emptiness. Then he walked back to Liverpool, slow, steady, resigned. Memories haunted Peter on the long road, his two lost loves, his father figure Egan, Lord Egerton Warburton's ridiculous fox hunts, marches in Swiss mountains, all distant fiction, again. Did any of it even happen at all? Now 24 years old, Peter felt an old man compared to the teenager who left his home in Prussia to change the world a decade ago. What a waste, he cried upward, as the stench and cotton dust of Liverpool's outskirts descended once more to taunt him with familiar cruelty.

He came to the docks. The sight of ships' masts lifted his heart, the lure of escape seized him. Second thoughts raced. This will all turn to shit, too. The boat would sink and he would drown. He'd end up shipwrecked on some island. Or he'd catch a plague in steerage, rotting to death with rats in the stinking hold. He paced the docks thinking, when he heard a voice just behind him as he passed someone by, so instantly recognizable he almost choked on it. "Spare a ha'penny?"

It was Paul.

"Penny for the poor?"

Peter turned, breathless. Paul held out his hat to a lady for a coin.

"God bless you, ma'am!"

Peter froze. Paul was a shell of the boy he had loved, now cutting a figure older even than Egan, and far more pathetic. Emaciated, drawn, covered in filth, his clothes rags, a shaggy beard, stinking of whiskey and his own excrement, Paul sat on a cotton bail, begging passers by holding out his hat. Peter whirled around looking away, overwhelmed by two days of relentless hell, and now this. Now what.

The night Paul left Arley Hall to meet Peter at The Swan, within minutes of his arrival a gentleman offered him to be his butler, conditioned that Paul must leave with him that night. Trap sprung, Paul promised himself he'd go back to get Peter again, but the gentleman, of course, forbade it. Paul spent two years as the gentleman's kept boy, finally running away into the slums, which consumed him. He turned tricks to survive. He tried returning to Arley Hall once, but was now a poison. One never returns to the aristocracy one abandons; a lesson Peter learned many times. Word got to Paul how lovely The Swan had become with its new, sophisticated barkeep; but Paul was too ashamed to return to Peter. Opium dens erased months of Paul's life, on and off, never knowing what year it was, day of the week, time of day. Now a begging drunk at the docks, Paul was so awful to behold he repelled human contact.

Imagining the life Paul must have lived since they left Arley Hall, Peter trembled. Taking a deep breath, steadying himself, Peter stepped in front of Paul to be seen, removing his hat. Paul looked up, recognizing Peter only after he begged him for money.

"Spare a...", Paul paused. Then Paul stood up. A brief moment of muted joy flared between them, fizzled to an ember, then to dust in no time at all.

"I waited for you," Peter whispered in shocked sorrow. Paul turned to walk away. "Paul wait!" Peter shouted. Paul stopped, didn't look back, just stood still, waiting. Peter ran to him, reaching into the cash box in his haversack for a fistful of money. Facing Paul, Peter dropped the coins into Paul's hat. Paul looked at it, gripped the hat tight, and ran off.

Totally drained inside and out, Peter sat down on the cotton bail Paul just abandoned. He gazed at the masts on the ships. Seagulls cried out in the sky, travelers mingled, the sea breeze blew through him. Peter's mind was empty, like his world. An hour, then another, passed, Peter motionless, in a daze. Finally, a deep breath, then nothing else to do but calculate how far away the cash box could take him. Not far at all; he'd put nearly all his money into Paul's hat.

"Perfect," Peter laughed, gallows humor all that was left. "Apprentice shipsmith needed," read a sign posted at a ship bound for America. There was no going back. Peter convinced the ship's blacksmith he was good with a hammer, and his crossing was arranged. On the long voyage, landing a hammer onto an anvil, over and over, chased the sadness away, as The Ghost's breath filled the ship's sails to take Peter Marks to America.

6 TOBY

Bred for export

By the time he was born in 1842, Toby's value as a slave resided no longer in his labor but his body, like a calf born of oxen. His mother was privately held corporate stock, owned by a shareholder who split the stock, then sold the split, to double the investment. It did not matter where Toby was sold to, just that he would be sold, preferably as quickly as possible, to minimize the cost of his maintenance. This is because Toby was born on a plantation outside Yorktown, Virginia, where labor to harvest tobacco had been rapidly losing value since well before Toby's mother was born.

The Lee family of York County owned the tobacco plantation where they bred Toby for export.

Unrelated to the more famous Lee family of northern Virginia, they became known as "the Peninsula Lees", descendants of the earliest colonists who were granted 1,000 acres by King James I in 1618. For 200 years, on land their king stole then handed to them at no cost, peninsula plantation owners near Yorktown like the Lees proceeded to suck the rich alluvial soil nearly dry. Virginia tobacco burned "sweet" into the lungs of the English aristocracy, prized across the British Empire as the most sophisticated to smoke. Its labor-intensive cultivation required attention to every detail; the weather, the seed, the water, but most of all the soil. Slave import trade boomed, bringing Toby's ancestors on slave ships to rape the land of its sweetness so lords and ladies could experience it in their parlors, wafting around them like the breath of Lucifer from the bowels of hell, as they built their empire.

Alas, tobacco is a hungry plant. Each year's new crop depleted more of the nutrients in the Virginia Peninsula soil responsible for such delicate perfection in its smoke. Their labor costless, never paid for, slaves proliferated. The more tobacco more slaves harvested, the more the soil deteriorated. As their royalty granted acres passed from one generation to the next, more land was inevitably left fallow, abandoned to grow thick forests, because less and less of it could produce the prized leaf. Toby's mother was born on the Lees' plantation just as it became clear to every plantation owner in Virginia's tidewaters they all had too many slaves. Ever the good business minds, the Lees soon switched to another slave trade; exports of the slaves themselves.

The same inexorable pattern developed in every cotton and tobacco growing region of the original thirteen colonies of America, from its founding. Too many slaves for too few crops from fewer and fewer fertile plots, none of it ever paid for, demanded new markets be found to export a new commodity, human beings, lest those factors of production become sunk costs, sucking on profit margins with their every breath. The raw material changed from cottonseeds and land, to mothers and fathers, the new product from cotton bales and tobacco leaves to children, the profit margin from unpaid labor and land to a baby's birth. Plantation families in the Virginia Peninsula soon began leaving their royal grants, farmed into forests on dead land by generations, migrating westward and south to find new fertile ground to pillage after not paying for it. By Toby's birth in 1842, the Peninsula Lees' "farm" was one of very few large tobacco plantations remaining near Yorktown, having become less a family of planters than of breeders.

Toby's mother grew up watching families ripped apart, sent one by one to auction blocks, bought by brokers who took them south and west to the newer, emptier stolen lands less depleted. As a little girl, one day she had a friend in the tobacco field next to her, the next day her friend was gone. One day, her own father disappeared, her mother's heartbreak joining the wails of mothers losing their children, days and nights filled with inconsolable grief as she grew up. Then her own mother was sold, leaving her alone, wondering where she too would be sold, south or west, to work fields not yet plundered by the voracious cotton and tobacco plants. She became pregnant with Toby by pure chance, his father too being sold onward before Toby was born.

She cried throughout her pregnancy, able to calm herself in only one way. She would gather up remnants of old slave clothing, torn bits and pieces of negro cloth falling in tatters from the slaves in the field. After her day bent over tobacco plants, she would sort them carefully in the slave cabin, by color. Darker strips here, lighter strips there. The slaves in her cabin at first thought she'd gone insane, collecting bits of trash. Her purpose soon became clear. The Peninsula Lees had long ago deduced that slaves would repair their own clothing, so slave quarters were equipped with threads, thimbles, and needles. Once she had a sufficient pile of scraps, she began sewing them together into a striped blanket, for her baby.

To assist, the other slaves commenced gathering bits of negro cloth, too. Two of the ladies, Belle and Jean, even began helping Toby's mother sew the strips together in the evenings.

"This gonna be some blanket!" Belle declared one night, stitching away.

"Too big," Jean said.

"Keep a-goin'," Toby's mother insisted.

"Babies grow, Jean, hate to tell ya," Belle chuckled, holding up a section to inspect it. "Think I need a few darker patches."

"Here," Toby's mother said, reaching into her pile of meticulously sorted cloth. There were no colors other than dark and less dark. Stained and less stained. But if carefully chosen and aligned, stripes resulted. It was something they could do for themselves, and for this child, when so little they did gave any value to anyone other than the Peninsula Lees, or their customers.

Inspecting the strip of cloth from the pile, Belle declared, "That'll do." And so it went, night after night, until an enormous blanket, beautiful to behold, sat folded away in a corner of the slave quarters, awaiting Toby's birth. His mother put out of her mind that this child, too, would be sold from her someday. Kept uneducated like every slave, she could not know why slaves got sold, why the forests around the plantation grew denser, wider, and thicker with underbrush, nor why tobacco fields were getting smaller, less of it to pick and bale. She just knew that within her grew a baby who would be with her only a short time, without any doubt. Thus, she named her baby after the plant that broke her back, and her heart.

Toby was born a very sick baby, so constantly ill

his mother wondered if God above decided Toby should die as a child to avoid growing old enough to work, thus sold. Swaddled in the striped blanket since birth, Toby's endless bouts just to breathe kept his mother awake every night, and out of the fields most days to tend to her wheezing little one. The Lees' slave master allowed it for a while. He knew the economics. If the child can live, let his mother keep him alive. Profit demanded it. But after two planting seasons, the slave master had enough. No one would buy this wheezing slave. "It" can hardly breathe, and the slave brokers who constantly preyed around like vultures knew it. No matter what age this child survived to be, the brokers knew "it" was sub-par product. Low quality. Word could spread far and wide that the Peninsula Lees were in the business of casting off damaged goods, which would destroy their ability to export product. The child was worthless, except to pick tobacco, or become one of the house slaves, and the Peninsula Lees long ago piled up too many of both.

In a blind rage during the harvest, Toby aged 2, the slave master snapped. His mother once again had stayed out of the fields to tend to the sick baby. Here was an opportunity to teach a lesson to any slave who dared think to care for a sick child ever again. The slave master charged into the slave quarters, took the baby from his mother's arms, tossed the striped blanket at him to shut him up, then dragged Toby's mother to a slave broker. The Peninsula Lees would damn well make their money back from their stock split, one way or another. No slave who saw Toby pulled from his mother that day ever forgot it. She fought, got whipped in front of everyone, then the slave master pulled her like a mule to a wagon as Toby wailed, tied her into the wagon, and drove her off the plantation into memory. All that was left behind for Toby was the striped blanket.

Mercifully, Toby was too young to remember that day as he grew older, except that he was so inseparable from his striped blanket, he needed it to sleep. The women in the slave quarters raised Toby together, in shifts, to make sure no one missed another day in the fields, all becoming Toby's "aunties". If a slave child can be spoiled at all, Toby's "aunties" managed it, especially Auntie Belle and Auntie Jean, who helped his mother stitch that blanket of his. First, they kept the blanket spotlessly clean. They told Toby as he grew up his mama went to heaven, and was happy there. Then, they made sure Toby was a favorite of the Lee ladies in the big house. Auntie Belle took care of that. She was the field slave who most interacted with the house slaves, through the kitchen. Through Auntie Belle, Toby became indispensable as a deliverer of fresh groceries to the kitchen hands. Thus, Toby was regularly assigned some of the easiest tasks any slave boy could hope for. Nestled into this nook, Toby could survive.

The slave boy in stripes

Branded as flawed by the slave master, had Toby been born just a few years later, the growing desperation of the Peninsula Lees to cut their losses might have ended Toby's high cost life with a noose. Efforts to halt the expansion of slavery in the west had halved the available export market with the Missouri Compromise in 1850, drawing a line from the Mississippi River to the Pacific Ocean, to the north of which no slave could be exported. By then, Toby was eight years old, had largely outgrown his childhood sickliness, and was now rather clever at using his presumed flawed status in his favor. One foot in the field slave quarters, the other in the kitchen with the house slaves, Toby learned the ways of both, effortlessly flitting between the two worlds, growing into an exceptionally charming little boy. Even the Lee ladies noticed this kitchen slave who lived with the field slaves. It wouldn't be long before the Peninsula Lees made little Toby a house slave, and even though this is precisely what Auntie Belle had hoped, the prospect worried her to no end.

The problem was the striped blanket. Without it, Toby was irritable, ornery, quick to anger on a very short fuse; not the sort of house slave the Peninsula Lees would tolerate in their mansion for very long at all. After a day of errands to and from the fields to the kitchen, Toby would run into the slave quarters to dive straight to his striped blanket, lying with it until he fell asleep, exhausted from controlling himself to behave. One autumn night, Auntie Belle and Auntie Jean got to arguing about it.

"That boy and that blanket," Auntie Belle worried as Toby snored in the corner, wrapped in the stripes.

"We done spoiled him," Auntie Jean replied matter of factly, darning a sock.

"What else we s'posed to do??"

"Coulda just let him be," Auntie Jean snapped.

"And let him end up in the fields coughin' and hackin' all day? He'd be dead by now, Jeannie."

"*Shoulda* just let him be."

"They'da hung him just to keep him from gettin' all them other slaves sick!"

"He outgrew it. He don't cough no more."

"You're the one who washed that blanket clean his whole life, Jeannie, don't you forget it."

"Ain'ta lettin' no child sleep in some filthy rag."

"You coulda switched in a different blanket every now and then, Jean."

Auntie Jean laughed. "You see a pile o' blankets here?"

"Coulda gave him yours."

"You seen him cry without that thing!"

"And whose idea was that???"

"What idea."

"Tyin' him to that blanket his whole life!"

"Baby needs a blanket every night, don't it?" Round and round they argued as Toby slept, wearing each other out. "Shoulda seen this a-comin', Jean. Now he can't be away from that thing!"

"That boy and stripes..." Auntie Jean muttered. Finally, Auntie Belle had an idea. She slept on it.

"Come here, Toby," Auntie Belle demanded first thing in the morning the next day. "I'ma gonna measure you." With a string, Auntie Belle took Toby's leg measurements.

"I don't need no pants, Auntie Belle," Toby complained.

"You need *different* pants, and you're a getting' em," Auntie Belle instructed, dragging the string up one of Toby's legs, down the other. That day in the fields, Auntie Belle sought out Auntie Jean with the news. "You and me sewin' that boy striped pants startin' tonight." Auntie Jean shook her head, bent over tobacco plants.

"You really somethin', Belle."

"Gonna see if they work like that blanket."

"If they do, then what? He gonna outgrow em quick."

"Sew him new ones."

Like Toby's mother did before he was born, Auntie Belle and Auntie Jean commenced gathering bits of ragged cloth again. For weeks, they lovingly stitched Toby striped pants that nearly matched his blanket exactly. Toby watched them every night, excitement building. "You ready to try these on, boy?" Auntie Belle announced the night they were finished. Toby leapt into them, so thrilled with his new pants, his aunties had trouble separating him from those, too, proudly wearing his new striped pants every single day.

The slave boy in the striped pants became the talk of the gossipy Lee ladies overnight. The kitchen slaves teased Toby relentlessly, but by now, Toby could give as good as he got. He was growing up. The whole scheme had worked. Auntie Belle and Auntie Jean monitored Toby carefully for a month, quietly. Toby returned for bed less and less urgently every day, lingering in his striped pants longer than he needed to. He still needed the blanket to sleep, but soon Toby just came to bed every day like a normal tired boy, instead of a tortured boy needing his mother who was gone.

As Auntie Belle had expected, in spring 1852, the Peninsula Lees began grooming Toby to be a house slave, at age 10. Richard Decauter Lee, the reigning patriarch of the plantation, had decided to build himself a new mansion, and Toby would help build the house he would serve in. In between the back breaking hard labor of digging the foundation for the new house, Toby took occasional shifts in the old house to learn the ways of a house slave, the setting of tables, delivering of teas, drawing of baths, cleaning, washing, all of it. A favorite of the Lee ladies, Toby seemed destined to become part of the family, until Auntie Jean escaped the plantation in May, and it all fell apart.

Back to the fields

By 1852, the Fugitive Slave Act combined with the Missouri Compromise to make escaped slaves the most hunted commodity in American capitalism. Both combined with simple geography to make escaping slavery extra impossible on the Virginia Peninsula. You couldn't just walk across a border, as Maryland slaves could do to reach Mag Devit in Gettysburg. The Lee plantation near Yorktown sat far out on the peninsula toward the sea, beyond a series of choke points, which made a slave catcher's job far easier. Not much ground sat between the two mile wide James River to the south, and the two mile wide York River to the north. Any slave attempting to get through the peninsula to mainland Virginia had very little room for error. Even if an escaped slave made it through the peninsula, before them stretched hundreds of miles more of the rest of Virginia to be crossed, before reaching either the Ohio River far westward, or Maryland northward, another slave state to cross before reaching Pennsylvania. To attempt escape from the Peninsula Lees was sheer madness, so it rarely happened, more rare every passing year, let alone with success.

And yet, peninsula slaves still attempted escape, leaving behind them a trail of total misery sure to multiply once they failed. If they left families behind, the torment of knowing they'd never make it through haunted that family instantly, increasing daily, hourly. Then the slave would be brought back, dead or soon to be, as lessons would be made of them, every single time. Then came the retribution against anyone who may have helped them escape, whether they did help or not. All this was such a deterrent, in his 10 years of living by 1852, Toby heard of no slave who had tried to escape the Peninsula Lees, until Auntie Jean disappeared that May.

She had become possessed. If attempting escape was madness, Auntie Jean indeed had gone quite mad. Something in her felt evil. It gnawed at her, made her constantly nervous, twitchy, unable to be calm. Auntie Jean believed the Devil had entered her, filling her mind with horrible thoughts, ideas, and instincts. She felt more evil the more Toby worked at the new mansion's building site. Every day seeing Toby in the striped pants brought new hideous thoughts, demons dancing within her, goblins goading her toward Satan and his empty promises. Maybe she would kill Toby. Maybe he would kill her. Maybe she would kill herself, and him, then Auntie Belle. She couldn't shake it.

No "fight or flight" theory had yet been conceived, not even the concept of "mental illness", let alone reaching a hopelessly uneducated slave woman to help her understand her world. But surely this was Auntie Jean's torment. She had always struggled with raising Toby, since the day she watched the slave master rip Toby from his mother's arms. What could she do? Here was a 2 year old that needed a mother. It was Auntie Jean who took the best care of the striped blanket she helped his mother stitch, kept it spotless, sewed the holes, and tucked Toby under it every night. As the baby grew up, she asked herself every day why she didn't just "leave him be," instead of taking delicate care of the blanket that kept him from crying. Her last moment of happiness on the plantation was helping Auntie Belle sew Toby's striped pants, seeing him wear them with pride. Then the torment resumed in the opposite direction, Toby's stripes a double-edged blade into her soul.

She saw how the Lee ladies treated Toby, turning him into a house slave to entertain them in the striped pants Auntie Jean made with her own hands. In her mind, Auntie Jean could never separate Toby's survival from what happened to his mother, the direct line between her suffering and her son's life. That winter and spring, Toby's striped blanket and pants became salt on her wounds from a life in bondage, the lens through which sunlight concentrated onto a spot in her heart to burn a hole straight through her, a constant, daily reminder of the sickening world that could perpetuate such twisted sorrow, handed from one generation to another, never ending, ever. Unlike Auntie Belle, Toby's coming new life as a house slave brought Auntie Jean no joy. She helped raise Toby, and here he now was serving on his hands and knees the people who sold his mother away.

Was she jealous? This thought Auntie Jean did entertain, long enough to decide the Devil's doing pushed her to think such awful things. House slave versus field slave was no news on a plantation. Auntie Jean hated herself for going there, then hated the Lord for allowing the Devil into her heart, then herself again for blaming the Lord for her own weakness, and it all circled back into her mind, recycling, returning, consuming her. She could take it no longer. A slave attempted escape for a thousand reasons. For Auntie Jean, it was her final act of love toward Toby. She feared she'd hurt him, no idea how, or why, just that the Devil was at work within her. Like every slave, she considered escape many times in her life. Alone, any family sold away like so many others, Auntie Jean was just old enough to know the risk, still young enough to try. Her relentless inner turmoil that spring finally pushed her to try.

"Toby!" Auntie Belle shouted to wake him up that morning before sunrise. "Get outside and look for Auntie Jean!" He bounded awake, racing outside to run around aimlessly, shouting her name. Auntie Belle panicked and ran after him. "Shhhhh! Keep quiet!" It was too late. Toby may not have experience with a slave disappearing, but Auntie Belle sure did, so she knew that Toby was now connected to Auntie Jean's disappearance, if his panicked cries for her had been heard. They had. The search hounds started barking. The night watchmen had been alerted by Toby calling Auntie Jean's name.

Horror consumed Auntie Belle all morning. Toby went to the new mansion's building site to work as if nothing had happened. That first day passed with tension gripping every slave on the plantation. The old timers were certain Auntie Jean would be dragged back to be tortured to death in front of them. The younger slaves, like Toby, found themselves achingly torn between the same impending doom and boundless pride at Auntie Jean's daring attempt. When Toby returned from the mansion building site that night, Auntie Belle was curled up in a corner on her knees praying, weeping, bobbing back and forth in agony. Toby ran straight to her to console Auntie Belle, but it was no use. That night, Toby clung extra tightly to his striped blanket, but for the first time in his life, it was no use; he couldn't sleep. No one slept in any slave quarters the first night after Auntie Jean disappeared.

The next day arrived, and passed. Then another. Then a week. Each new day began with dread that would dissipate as evening arrived with the distinct even growing possibility that Auntie Jean had made it out. Could it be true? Did she really escape? After a month with no Auntie Jean, every slave on the Peninsula Lees' plantation practically burst with suppressed joy at the thought that she made it out. Except for Auntie Belle. She knew that if Auntie Jean made it, someone would pay for her escape, and the only slave they could tie to Auntie Jean's disappearance that morning was Toby, because he searched for her, like Auntie Belle told him to.

Thus ended Toby's brief period of grooming to be a house slave. The Lee ladies who once delighted in the charming slave boy in striped pants now only saw a potential usurper digging the foundations of their new mansion; a lousy, conniving, sneaky field nigger who could never be trusted. It did not matter no one could tie Toby to any escape plot. Some punishment had to be meted out, to someone, or every slave on the plantation would start plotting escape. One June morning, a month after Auntie Jean's disappearance, they whipped 10-year-old Toby senseless before the rest of the slaves, because he called her name the morning she escaped.

Auntie Belle's relief that they didn't just hang him overpowered her. She tended to Toby's whipped back that night as he wept like the baby he was when his mother was taken from him. "I'm so sorry, Toby!" Auntie Belle cried, "I shouldn't have asked you to look for her, it's all my fault!" Toby hugged Auntie Belle so hard they both lost their breath for a moment.

"Don't cry, Auntie Belle," Toby consoled through his tears. "I'll be alright, and Auntie Jean is free." From that night onward, Toby didn't need the striped blanket so much anymore except to keep him warm in winter, and when he grew out of the striped pants, no new ones were stitched.

7 JOHN FISHER

The First Minnesota's path bends toward a certain farm

If no one ever knew he existed, John Fisher would have felt that a success. Born a slave around 1800, none know where, John Fisher inherited his drive and determination from his mother, who carried her boy from slavery to freedom one night. Little kids don't know they're penniless lawbreakers on the run; they just know it's an adventure, because that's how Mama made it. Mama didn't even let Little Johnnie know hunger on the journey to Pennsylvania, although Fisher would recall he got tired of eating found rotting apples. His only memory of escaping slavery - in fact, his first memory - was the journey's darkness. Walking at night, days were in cellars, crawl spaces, barn lofts, anywhere but visible, the escape leaving Fisher forever with a quiet, nameless fear of being seen.

Fisher's childhood memories of daylight began with Gettysburg, where Mama settled down as a housemaid, here and there. Although she couldn't, Mama made sure her son learned to read and write. Newspapers filled the boyhood moments between collecting firewood, delivering laundry, fieldwork, things a little former slave kid could do for pay. Young Fisher took to farms, growing up tall and strong, minding his own business, staying unseen.

When Mama's church, St. Paul's AME Zion, began the Slave Refuge Society to help runaways using Gettysburg as a key route north, Fisher's first memories of darkness were triggered. He never attended the meetings, letting folks find his mother after church for advice, guidance about this trail, or that one. Even as they both grew old, Mama kept her Little Johnnie safe from those memories, helping the Society on her own without ever speaking of it to her son. John just worked, read newspapers, found farms that needed hands. He so diligently kept to himself that around town, the notion that Fisher's mother fled slavery with a little child in tow seemed a rumor.

But exist John Fisher did, when one spring day in 1851, Mama was on her way to her heavenly reward. Fisher held her hand in his workman fingers, sitting beside her bed in his new cabin. He'd begun tenant farming on a plot slowly rising up the eastern slope of

Cemetery Ridge from the Taneytown Road to the crest. To convince Mama he'd be fine after she was gone, that he'd found a place to settle where he needn't be seen, he made quick work that spring of the trees on the wide parcel, building himself a log cabin near the Taneytown Road. The tiny house where she died convinced Mama that Little Johnnie would be able to exercise the option in his tenancy to buy the plot for himself, someday. That hope made Mama smile as she breathed her last in the cabin on Taneytown Road.

Fisher spent the summer after Mama died farming that plot on Cemetery Ridge like he'd never worked before. Scraping a living off his own piece of land had become less a dream to finally fulfill than a promise to his Mama he would damn well keep. At least 50 years old by autumn 1851, who could tell, Fisher figured a three or four years' crops carefully budgeted, proceeds saved, food canned, stored, pickled, smoked...and he could buy the land. Each minute's work on every inch of that ground toward getting his hands on that deed, he thought of Mama. He spent that first cold winter of 1851-1852 huddled alone in the cabin, surviving on what he'd manage to stockpile, reading by his stove to keep warm, each log on the fire in the stove carefully counted out, burned long and slowly, conserved, measured.

It all changed in January, 1852, a panicked knock at his door one snowy evening nearly throwing Fisher off his rocking chair. A burst of snow blew open the cabin door and in shivered a frozen solid 16-year-old Mag Devit, dragging behind her nothing but trouble. In a flash, he saw Mama laughing down from the Pearly Gates, "I got you! Hee hee! I GOT you!" Having spent his entire life avoiding the route Mama walked him to freedom upon, here it now was, about to consume the rest of his days. All Fisher could do was rub his forehead, staring at the floor.

"You Ol' Lady Fisher's boy, John, ain't ya??" Mag blurted, shaking snow off, warming by Fisher's stove. "We met at church. I'm so sorry she's gone, she was such a lovely lady..." And on, and on Mag went, in one of Fisher's ears, out the other, Mag oblivious to Fisher's mind racing forward to immediately obsess over the endless flood of problems Mama sent down to him from above, through Mag.

"Evenin', Miss Devit," Fisher moaned to himself. Mag helped herself to a chair.

"You don't mind a little visit, do you?" Mag peeled her bundled layers away, helping herself to Fisher's hospitality for the night, snapping Fisher back to reality.

"I suppose...," he began, glaring at Mag, "...you think this is a hotel?"

Mag batted her eyes, turning on the charm, "Now, Mr. Fisher, you wouldn't put a girl out in the cold, would you?" Fisher stewed.

"You just carry on home now."

"Can't. Slave catchers can't be seein' no footie prints in that snow, you know that." Fisher flashed back to Mama carrying him in a bag on her back to insure only one set of footprints in the mud on their way to freedom. He caught his breath. A pause fell. Mag stopped moving, suddenly unsure of herself.

Fisher stood up, heaving. He turned to Mag. "I don't own this here land, Mag," slow anger percolating. "Don't you start makin' no plans here."

"I see." Mag crossed her legs. Time to get down to business. "Well, you'll just have to own it pretty soon then."

"What??"

"You heard me, ya old coot! Quit beatin' around this here bush." Fisher paced his tiny cabin. Wind outside howled as Fisher kicked the little snow pile Mag dragged in.

"What the hell you doin' out on a night like this anyway?" Fisher barked.

"You know what I's up to," Mag sneered, "and you know I need a cut through from the Taneytown Road, and that's this here farm. That tenant before you almost SHOT me, and well, now you're here. So, way I sees it, you need to buy this here farm, Fisher!"

Stunned silence slammed Fisher back into his rocking chair. He rocked back and forth, faster each time. "You see money fallin' in that snow??"

"I knew your Mama, bless her soul, and she didn't raise no damn fool..."

Fisher raised a finger. "You keep my mama's name out your mouth, little girl." A clash of titans was afoot.

"Don't you sass me!" Mag suddenly sounded like his Mama. Fisher just looked up at the ceiling, exasperated, Mag undeterred. "Them slaves don't run much in this weather, but in spring, them fields gonna have slaves runnin' 'cross 'em like rabbits, most every night, along with ME, whether you like it or not, and you might as well be ownin' this land when they come runnin'."

All business, Mag sat back in her chair, taking off her shoes wet with snow, to lay against the stove to dry. She crawled up to the cabin loft, and was sound asleep in no time. Mag kept Fisher awake all night in disbelief at how loud a teenaged girl could snore, doing the figures in his head how to buy the farm ahead of schedule.

"Mama," he whispered to the heavens in bed, "you sure got me this time."

A puppy adopts John Fisher

It would become known down the years as "the copse of trees", but to John Fisher by 1852, it was a shady resting place with a view. One plot north from his, at the crest of Cemetery Ridge, the trees' owner, Peter Frey, accepted they would become a gathering spot, perched as they were with a grand view westward to the rolling mountains of Pennsylvania west of Gettysburg. The Ghost, possessing the patience of the seasons, reposed in the trees' rustling branches, or the color of their leaves in autumn. In summer the trees drew picnicking families. In just over a decade, the dead would claim the "copse" for eternity, and make Basil Biggs a lot of money.

The term "copse" was coined for the trees by John Badger Bachelder, the father of Gettysburg historical preservation, whose focus on that spot would never dim. Robert E. Lee on July 3, 1863, called them a "clump" when he identified the trees as the point of convergence for George Pickett's final charge. After the war, they fell to African American Basil Biggs, an Underground Railroad colleague of Mag and Fisher, perhaps the first venture capitalist of the battle. A farmer and veterinarian, Biggs earned a healthy nest egg re-burying battlefield dead for months after the battle. With that money, Biggs managed to purchase the plot with the trees from Peter Frey. Ever industrious, in 1869, Biggs decided to cut down the trees on his new plot for firewood, when fortune struck again. A passing gentleman, Bachelder, surveying the battlefield that was now his life's obsession, was horrified at Biggs hacking away at what were now holy relics, asking Biggs, "Do you know what these trees are?"

A sort of squire patrician landed gentry of military pedigree who married well, Bachelder was a yeoman landscape painter in New Hampshire when the war broke out. Uninterested in bleeding for his country despite his military education, he became a camp follower of the Army of the Potomac, to paint the fields they bled across. Gettysburg consumed the rest of Bachelder's life the day the battle commenced. By the time he met Biggs cutting down the "copse" in 1869, Bachelder was Gettysburg's unofficial keeper, leading preservation efforts through the Gettysburg Battlefield Memorial Association. Soon after the war, Bachelder lunched near Biggs' trees on Cemetery Ridge with a former Confederate general, who confirmed the trees to Bachelder as Lee's objective for Pickett's charge. *Voila* - Basil Biggs' lucky day.

Bachelder convinced Biggs in 1869 his land was far more valuable than the firewood from the trees upon it, so sniffing opportunity in the breeze, Biggs stopped cutting them, then put the screws to Bachelder. A years long legal battle over price ensued, Biggs holding out against the GBMA for every red cent. No one knows how many of those trees came down before Biggs stopped cutting them, nor which of them John Fisher sat underneath to rest that spring of 1852.

Fisher carried a rocking chair up to the trees on the crest after a long day of spring clearing to watch the sunset, as storm clouds loomed rumbling on the western horizon. Down the slope of the ridge Fisher could see the Emmitsburg Road fade southward, Nicholas Cordori's farm along it, and to the northwest the tiny shack on Abraham Brien's farm where Mag Devit lived with her mother. The sky grew orange as thunder settled ominously over Fisher rocking his weary bones back and forth. A ruckus erupted at Mag's shack. Waving her arms like an angry mother, Mag chased a tiny stray dog, barking at it louder than it barked at her. "Hee hee!" Fisher squealed, in a high enough pitch that the puppy heard, snapping her stare up the ridge at him.

"Got me again, Mama," Fisher said to himself as the puppy bolted up the ridge to begin her very own Cemetery Ridge charge at the "copse". As her charge began, Fisher wondered if he had time, patience, even room for a dog at the tenant farm he did not yet own. The bundle of fur hurtled herself toward him, bounding along, when lightning struck in the western hills, its thunder clapping so loud Fisher almost fell out of his rocking chair. The puppy was undeterred. Nothing could stop this charge up Cemetery Ridge at those trees, except the puppy's own clumsiness. She stumbled, rolling into a swale of ground, disappearing. Fisher stood up to look, briefly concerned, when the puppy bolted out of the swale, hopping faster, leaping over the next swale, onward. Thunder roared. The Ghost was at work again. Fisher squatted down to greet his new friend as the puppy neared, throwing herself onto Fisher. Lightning ripped across the sky.

"Well, well, little girl," Fisher chuckled between licks across his face. "What should we call a dog rollin' out of a flash of lightning?" That was it. "Flash! Hello, Flash!" Inseparable instantly, Fisher and Flash played on the ground under the trees as the heavens opened up a torrent to the west. "Come on, girl, let's get inside," Fisher announced, picking up the rocking chair, and racing down the eastern slope toward his cabin, Flash hurrying behind, having found a home.

Mama tells Mag the news

Mama waddled home exhausted after a long day delivering laundry in town just as Mag chased off the puppy. "Storm a-rollin' in!" Mama declared as Mag battened down the hatches. "Whose dog was that?"

"Think it wandered over from Codori's farm...looks like Fisher's now," Mag chuckled.

"Oh, that reminds me, let's sit a while." Mama announcing a sit down was no joke, always. By 1852, Mag was 16 years old, no longer a little girl, and had been running slaves two of those years. She knew the drill. If Mama wanted to "sit a while", that meant putting the kettle on, brewing her some tea, then slave runnin' business. Spring meant slaves would be runnin' soon. Kettle meant news. Over just such a kettle, Mama taught Mag about the cut-through between their shack and McAllister's Mill; the woods between the Baltimore Pike and Taneytown Road. From there, Mama knew Mag liked to cut over the ridge, because Mama did just that plenty of times her self. Mama knew that land, that Peter Frey owned it, and just how critically helpful it would be for a friendly to come into one of those plots, instead of some ornery old shotgun toting tenant farmer paying Mr. Frey rent. When Mag had to stay a night in John Fisher's cabin that winter, well, Mama set out to move a few mountains. Like all mothers do.

"Now then...I was in town today..." Mama began, and Mag smiled to herself. That meant Mama had been workin' some angle for weeks. "...and I ran into Judge Ziegler." Mag suppressed laughter. Mama never just "ran into" some county judge. Mag set the table for tea, the kettle on the stove, and the storm blew in, battering the tiny shack. "You'll never believe what Judge Ziegler told me today, Mag!"

"Mama," Mag said sitting down, "I ain't a little girl no more."

Just then, Mama knew, in the look on her

daughter's face. Taking off her shoes, she paused. For the first time, she finally realized she could tell the whole story, instead of hiding this and that from her daughter. Her baby had grown up. Mama began to weep. Mag watched her mother try to hide it for a tense moment, then instincts kicked in, so she lunged to hug her mother, hold her, and let her cry, just like Mama did for Mag as a baby.

"I never wanted you runnin' no slaves!" Mama cried. Mag rocked Mama in her arms, sharing the chair, rain and wind howling. "I'm so sorry, Mag! So, so sorry..."

"Don't you be cryin'," Mag said, repeating her mother's words from a lifetime of hearing them. "Now you just tell me about your day in town." It would be a while before Mama collected herself, so Mag just held her, rocking, until the kettle whistled.

"You know I love you, little girl," Mama cried.

"And I love you."

"This slave runnin' is terrible business, Mag."

"God's work, Mama. God's work."

"I thought someday they'd be free before you grew up..." Mama trembled. "Someday never come..."

"I learned from the best, Mama, so you got nothin' to worry about, ya hear?"

"Maybe that someday will come," Mama whimpered.

"Come on, now, time for tea." Mag got up off the chair to take the step to the wood stove, so Mama got herself together. Turning with the kettle, Mag saw Mama smiling, finally, wiping tears.

"One lump or two?" Mag joked.

Mama shared her first adult joke with her daughter. "This gonna take two lumps, baby girl." They shared womanly laughter as Mag poured the kettle, and the news broke.

"Now you listen here!" Mama wagged her finger. "When you're runnin' slaves, sometimes, we have to do certain things, Mag, things we don't talk about."

Mag knew instantly. "You didn't!"

"Well, not today anyway..."

"WHAT?"

"Calm yourself down, young lady, some things you do one time, and they last a very long while. *You understand?*" Oh, the wheels that turned in Mag's mind. She reeled. Who? When? How? Was it...she couldn't speak. Mama spared her the agony.

"Many years ago, before you were born, Judge Ziegler and I...well...let's just leave it at that."

"Oh, we gonna leave it at that, allright," Mag said.

"And ever since, if I need somethin' real bad...he's very kind!" Mag stared in awe at her mother stirring sugar into her tea. "Besides, ain't no judge wants people knowin' he been with a nigga."

"Why, you devil!"

Mama was all business. "Took me a while, but John Fisher owns that farm you cut across, Mag."

"How the HELL?"

Mama got very insistent, teaching. "Judges in this county can pull many strings, young lady, and you need to *remember that*." Mag fell back in her chair, beyond thinking. "Turns out one of them strings is gettin' Fisher's landlord to sell." Mama sipped her tea, very proudly.

The Ghost warms a slave in Fisher's cabin

Fisher never learned why his landlord, just in time for spring planting in 1852, up and decided to lower the price of exercising his option from four years' wheat crop to one. Fisher just felt something supernatural was at work from the day the deal closed, so assumed it was Mama from heaven helping him along. Flash was just a signal from her above; every farm needs a dog. Thus, The

Ghost began making sure John Fisher was present the day the First Minnesota arrived on his plot at sunrise, July 2, 1863. At every crossroads the next decade, The Ghost guided Fisher's presence to permanence.

Standing in a cloudy morning's chilly April mud, Flash getting her paws filthy chasing squirrels, Fisher surveyed his new domain, deciding what to farm for subsistence rather than just a cash crop of wheat to pay rent with. Over the crest of Cemetery Ridge appeared Mag, marching down the slope. Fisher erupted laughing.

"What's so funny?" Mag shouted from halfway up the ridge. Bent over possessed by laughter, Fisher caught his breath to yell up the ridge.

"The Lord works in mysterious ways, Mag!"

"Word is you own this here plot now!"

"Ask and you shall receive, Miss Devit!" Warm hugs of congratulations gave way to Mag's recognition of the new mutt.

"Is this that dog from Codori's farm?"

"Don't know where she's from, but she's here now...come on Flash, say hello to Mag!" Flash had already learned the hard way Mag wasn't all that friendly, so shied away. "She don't like you, Mag," Fisher chuckled.

"This a good place for a dog," Mag thought aloud. "Gonna need some chickens, Fisher."

"Maybe some pigs. A cow. Gotta plant half the plot with wheat for a season to pay it off." Flash tore off after a bird. The wheels began to turn in Mag's head.

"Slave runnin' season about to pick up, too, Fisher," Mag thought out loud. Despite knowing Mag would seize opportunity everywhere it arose, Fisher was still irritated.

"This ain't your land, Mag, you got that?"

"Oh, no, of course!" Mag joked, watching Flash chase critters across the field. A watchdog, Mag wondered. Perfect.

"Ain't mine yet, either. Gotta sell one more wheat crop."

"Ya don't say?" Mag quietly felt awe for her mama's negotiating skill. "This autumn then?"

"If not sooner," Fisher replied.

"Soon enough," Mag decided. Flash barked in the distance at a mole, or something. Mag suddenly liked this dog. Fisher paced, knowing Mag's agenda. In futility, Fisher tried to limit what he most certainly knew would be limitless risk.

"Here's the deal, Mag."

"Now we're talkin'."

"You can cut across here anytime with any slaves, day or night, just be careful 'bout it..."

"You know I will, Fisher!"

"...and don't you bring just any ol' swamp nigga into my house, ya hear?"

"Slaves probably showin' up in the next week or so," Mag pondered. Fisher sighed with frustration. Mama's hand was in this, somehow, Fisher knew it. He looked at Mag, her arms crossed in front of her, watching Flash run around. Fisher hated even saying it, but he knew what she wanted to hear.

"In a pinch," Fisher struggled to get out, "you can come in the cabin, if there's trouble."

There would always be trouble, starting that night. Mag turned up with a slave, barging into Fisher's cabin as he read his Bible by his hot stove to chase away the spring night's chill. The commotion woke up Flash from Fisher's bed, barking.

"McAllister's Mill full up with slaves a-runnin'!" Mag announced, walking in like she owned the place. "Spring is here, Fisher!"

"You couldn't wait ONE DAMN DAY!?" Fisher exclaimed, slamming his Bible on the table. The slave shivered in the doorway, afraid of the dog. "Get in here!" Fisher yelled at the slave, glaring at Mag as the slave scurried to the stove to warm himself, Flash clumsily hurling herself at a new friend.

"Some watchdog you got, Fisher," Mag laughed, looking down at the puppy trying to get the slave's attention.

"Ooooh, I oughta..." Fisher fumed. "I told you I don't own this land 'til I sell that wheat crop!"

Mag got sassy, wagging her finger, "Now, now...Just a little test! He's stayin' at ol' man Brien's farm, we just a-passin' through, so you can cool your raggedy old head."

"Did I pass your little test, Miss Devit?"

"You let us in didn't ya?" Mag pulled a treat out of her pocket for Flash, some suet McAllister gave her at the mill, for just such an occasion. "Come here, girl, leave that boy alone, he's scared enough."

Fisher turned to see the slave warming himself at the stove.

"You must be alright since my dog here don't seem to mind."

"Here, give her this," Mag said to the slave, handing him the suet. As Flash gobbled the suet from his hands, the slave turned to Fisher. "Thank you, sir, thank you, and God bless you."

Fisher gestured toward Mag. "She's a real piece of work, but you're in good hands, boy."

The slave smiled, as The Ghost breathed on the fire in the stove to warm all the souls in John Fisher's cabin.

GHOSTS OF PLUM RUN

8 ANTON WALDMANN

A German poaches an Irishman's fiddler

St. Paul's boom peaked just as Jacob Amos laid the foundation stones for Anton Waldmannn's lager bier saloon in summer 1857. The two immigrants had become fixtures in St. Paul's burgeoning German community; Amos a stonemason of the ancient Darmstadt masonry guild, Waldmannn a fuel wood seller to the steamboats, his shed at the Upper Landing, the final stop north on the Mississippi River. Ever ahead of the game, the entrepreneurial Waldmann sensed the boom's choking river traffic couldn't last; soon, railroads would come. Thus, Waldmann's "Deutschstum", or "Germanness", took the place of wood sales as his new enterprise.

Born a peasant subject of King Maximilian I Joseph of Bavaria in 1823, Anton Waldmann's parents Johann and Anna Maria were tenant farmers in Kleinostheim, a small village southeast of Frankfurt in Lower Franconia. They named their second child Leonhard, not Anton, at his Catholic baptism. In 1825, when baby Leonhard was 2, King Max's son Ludwig ascended the throne of Bavaria. His Royal Majesty Ludwig I carried on kinging until the 1848 revolution demoted him to a lord. It was all very messy. While kinging, Ludwig collected mistresses, one of whom was an Irish dancer calling herself Lola, who had such a hold on Ludwig he made her a countess. No Irish dancer ever had so much power in Bavaria. Such untoward palace intrigues outraged conservative Catholics, who saw the revolutions suddenly boiling up all around them in 1848 as an opportunity to dispatch this cunning usurper. Within 2 months of the first protests in Bavaria in February, 1848, Ludwig I had abdicated in March. Like so many of the brief pyrrhic successes of the 1848 revolution, a new king ascended anyway; Ludwig's son, another King Max, the second. Leonhard Waldmann by then was a 25-year-old shoemaker.

In 1853, Leonhard immigrated to America with his new name, Anton. Like so many German immigrants who settled in St. Paul after 1848, cleaning their slate with a new name was born of a thousand reasons, not a single one of which could ever truly be known, which was the point. Perhaps he just sought new opportunity in

America, or, as Peter Marks, perhaps he had to flee the noose. Perhaps he despised the revolutionaries. As a Catholic peasant in Bavaria, Leonhard was just a trifle too old at 25, raised a bit too conservatively, to join 1848's rabble in the streets, let alone their army marching in quixotic futility across Germany for a year. Perhaps he'd made boots for student revolutionaries to march in, or their pursuers. Perhaps his Catholic sensibilities forced him one day, in a fit of piqued indiscretion, to publicly throw his lot in with the revolutionaries for whom a royal scalp was worth a convenient temporary alliance with their arch rival conservative German Catholics disgusted by Irish temptress dancers scheming to become powerful countesses. Such European complications were so convoluted and contrived, best to forget them forever. Might have mattered to Leonhard the Bavarian cobbler peasant; it mattered nothing to Anton, now an American, where your name can change, your past erased, and a new life born with the mere stroke of a pen.

Somewhere in the American west, a German immigrant woman had smitten him, Wilhelmine Porth, born in another German town with impossibly ridiculous convolutions she too wanted forgotten. Mina and Anton wed, and came to St. Paul in 1856, the most perfect time and place on earth to start anew. Fortune smiled upon Anton and Mina from the moment they stepped onto a steamboat northward up the Mississippi River. On board, underneath their very feet, burned Anton's first big idea for his life in St. Paul; fuel wood, powering the big wheel pushing them upstream into Minnesota territory. Anton's timing was so perfect, even the spot where they disembarked, St. Paul's Upper Landing, the northern most port on the river, immediately became Anton's home. There, Anton built a woodshed, found a little house just a few hundred yards up the bluff for Mina in a freshly platted neighborhood of the frontier town, and set about collecting timber to sell. Again, timing smiled upon Anton and Mina, as the heaviest steamboat traffic in Minnesota history was about to descend upon St. Paul, bringing more German immigrants in every boat.

Therein lay Anton's next idea. Like every immigrant to America hoping to forget "the old country" in all its glorious byzantine absurdity, still, Anton was a German; that, he could neither erase nor run from. Might as well try to run from your own hair. Among the immigrants flooding St. Paul, every German's "Deutschstum" kept particular hold on their new life. Many were leftist revolutionaries in 1848, St. Paul their final stop in exile. From this radical core outward, German immigrant cultural and political sensibilities didn't fade into the American melting pot very much at all. They started music and reading societies, newspapers, theatre troupes performing in a lecture hall they erected with their own hands. They established a local "Turnverein", where gymnastics meshed with morals to keep a good German good. If they were at all religious, it was barely, and kept it to themselves. As Anton and Mina settled in, one particular German tradition Anton felt could be his next chapter, once steamboats burning wood lost out to railroads burning coal; something about Germans that everyone in St. Paul would embrace. Of course, that something was beer, specifically German lager bier, and the proper manner of drinking it.

By Anton's arrival in 1856, German breweries in St. Paul were big business, getting bigger. German lager's lighter, airy and delicate punch had begun to take hold of the American drinker's palate. Because it appeared to the eye as less alcoholic than whiskey and English ales, lager beer snuck right past the temperance old maids, often gaining legislative exception from the constant crusades against the demon drink. Thus, German lager breweries boomed and lager bier flooded St. Paul's saloons, whose reputation as a saloon town had been well earned long ago. Proliferating German saloons soon brought a little class and civilization to the entire affair. In Germany they were "gardens", more like festive family front rooms than booze bars; more lager than liquor, more warm fuzzies than wild wantonness. Food, music, poetry readings, lectures, debates; a full program of events and menus joined the prized golden lagers of Bavaria, the new brew hooking America. Thus, for his next act, Anton Waldmannn intended to perfect the German saloon in St. Paul, making every homesick German in St. Paul a "Waldmann's" regular customer. Anton would not add yet another rickety wood shanty stocked with moonshine to St. Paul. No, a stonemason, Jacob Amos, trained in the ancient German ways, would craft walls three feet thick to keep the Minnesota cold away, and inside, Anton's "Deutschstum" would take flight. It would be done right, or not done at all. There would be no saloon like it in the west.

Waldmannn did not much care for his fellow saloon keepers, who were English, French Canadian, or Irish, thus running groggy dens of iniquity, flimsy shacks filled with vulgar womanizing drunkards tossing back whiskey as if it were water, on empty stomachs no less, so also soon vomiting. This was the saloon tradition of Pig's Eye, as St. Paul used to be called; the unbridled drunkenness every temperance-hectoring busy body invoked when trying to ban alcohol, their first ban lasting all of six months in 1852. Even worse, the Irish saloon keeping set in particular was of the Know Nothing, slavery supporting, reactionary racist sort, Catholic moral hypocrites who wouldn't know a good beer if it rained down onto them. For Waldmann, his lager bier saloon would not just be an essential thread in this tapestry of German American immigrant life. It would be a contrast to St. Paul's wild saloon culture.

Thus, touring his competition on the lookout for a house musician during the boom summer of 1857 was very hard work for Waldmann, not relaxation. He endured it, like any thorough German would. Had to be done. As luck would have it, he had Seamus Dooley stacking his wood. Seamus now was one of the strapping young men who sawed and stacked Waldmann's 8-foot lengths of wood, 8'x8'x8' feet cubes at a time. On those cubes, "ranks" as they were called, Anton's keen eye for business kept close watch. Many fuel wood sellers on the Mississippi would cut that cube's corners, stacking the wood with spaces between, or filling the cube inside with softer, cheaper pine that burned too fast, rather than the slower burning hard wood the steamboat engineers demanded for maximum power. No rank from Anton Waldmann would have pine hiding in it, or air. This guarantee, combined with being the last stop north, New Orleans 2,300 miles to the south, afforded Waldmann a premium price. To ensure his woodstackers never once cut that corner, Waldmann would get to know his workers, such that he knew Seamus arrived in St. Paul on the *Doctor Franklin* that celebrated day years ago with his Uncle Paddy who taught violin. Everything seemed to go Anton Waldmann's way, all the time.

As Jacob Amos laid stone up the bank from his woodshed near the Upper Landing, Waldmann approached Seamus at the pile one day for guidance as to where he might hear Paddy Dooley at a saloon, or one of his students.

"Seamus, my good fellow, your Uncle Paddy teaches violin I understand."

"She plays at Hearn's Head Quarters most nights," Seamus said between sawing strokes. Waldmann was taken aback. How could one of his woodstackers know what he was up to?

"She?"

"Millie, my fiancé," Seamus paused sawing to wipe sweat off his brow and smile at Waldmann. "The finest fiddler in Minnesota territory, and everyone knows your saloon will need music!"

"But how do you ...?" By the boom summer of 1857, everyone seemed to know everyone else's business, because it was good business, lest anyone miss any...business. Word got around, about everything. So, Waldmann accepted that, like everyone else in St. Paul, his woodstacker was on the make, searching for schemes to cash in on, where word was getting around that Waldmann was about to open a saloon. Such an enterprising boy, Waldmann thought.

"I'll go with you to Shearn's and introduce you to Millie if you like, Mr. Waldmann." Seamus was coming out of his shell, the promise of striking it rich then marrying Millie had transformed Seamus instantly that summer, from a terrified little boy fleeing the famine and hating the world, to a Minnesota hustler about to be married to the most beautiful fiddler in the west. Waldmann had found the perfect guide, and to the perfect saloon, because stealing Shearn's fiddler out from under him was a delightful thought.

"Shearn's, you say?" Waldmann did not like Henry Shearn. "Yes, let's go to Mr. Shearn's, Seamus!"

That weekend, Waldmann stood smoking a pipe at the front of his half built stone saloon, Jacob Amos finishing up for the day as the sun set. They were not a hundred yards from each other, Shearn's and Waldmann's. Only 21 buildings were scattered across the undeveloped land called Leech's Addition, platted out on a map, but not yet exactly "streets", just, suggestions. Waldmann need only walk across some grass and weeds for a minute or two to meet his new fiddler. On the evening summer breeze, light fading, he could barely make out Millie's Irish reel beckoning.

"I never thought to listen more closely to that music coming from Shearn's," Waldmann said to Amos, in German. Amos gathered his tools away for the weekend, then looked over with Waldmann.

"Hard to tell from this distance, but I've heard it before, and seems quite competent," Amos added.

"One of my woodstackers is introducing me tonight," Waldmann said, puffing on his pipe.

"For the saloon?" Amos asked.

"If all goes well," Waldmann replied. The sun had gone, night setting in. "When did you say we might be able to open, Jacob?"

"I'd say we'll be done here by September," Amos declared. "Perhaps as late as October."

"So, around harvest time."

"Why yes, now that you mention it, harvest time," Amos smiled. Anton's timing never failed.

"Good. If that fiddler is as advertised, we shall open with music," Waldmann declared. "See you on Monday, Jacob." Waving goodnight, Waldmann walked across Leech's Addition toward the music on the night breeze, Millie's fiddle becoming easier to make out every step of the way. He found Seamus leaned against the doorpost, nodding at him as he approached. "Not bad!" Waldmann exclaimed at the door.

"That's nothin'," Seamus smiled. "Mr. Richard!" Seamus called out to Millie's father, entering with Waldmann. Shearn from behind the bar, ever vigilant, kept a hawk's eye on the stately German walking toward his violin player's father. Pleasantries exchanged, Papa, a cigar in hand, invited Waldmann to sit down to listen.

"Seamus!" Shearn shouted at the table, waving him over with a whisky in hand. "Who's that?" he asked Seamus before he even hit the edge of the bar, Seamus grabbing the shot glass.

"My boss," Seamus said, whisky down in an instant.

"Isn't he starting a saloon?"

Seamus became coy. "Maybe."

"A lotta nerve you have, Mr. Dooley!"

"She'll be my wife soon, Mr. Shearn, so her business is my business, not yours. Three whiskeys please?" Shearn stewed as he poured.

At the table, Waldmann listened carefully. "Paddy Dooley taught her to play like this??" Waldmann asked Papa. Papa dragged on his cigar, nodding. Seamus arrived with the drinks. Millie finished her reel, taking a bow to the slowly filling crowd.

Papa shouted at Millie, "Winter!" pointing at Waldmann, winking. Millie winked back; the first sheet music Mr. Dooley used to teach her minor key. Out it came, like the snowstorm that night in Mr. Dooley's America House hotel room, Seamus only 8 years old, crying himself to sleep, and The First Ghost of Gettysburg swirling winter gales against the window, into the hotel room, through her fiddle, then up to the heavens. Waldmann gaped in awe, swept away utterly. Papa waited grinning ear to ear, cigar smoke enveloping him, a trance over him, anticipating his daughter's worthy due, as she filled the shoddy walls with baroque.

"Vivaldi??" Waldmann gasped at Papa who raised the second whisky Seamus had already brought to the table.

"To Paddy Dooley!!" Not one to drink shots of whisky, Waldmann nevertheless joined. Business was business, after all.

"No one has heard Vivaldi in ages!" Waldmann declared. "How does an Irish fiddler bring his sheet music to St. Paul?? To teach it to a little girl??" Shearn watched from the bar, seething.

"The Lord works in mysterious ways, Mr. Waldmann!" Papa proclaimed. As Millie blew his mind, Waldmann did the sums in his head. It had been two record years in a row for steamboats in St. Paul, and selling them fuel. Money would be no object. Bargaining commenced.

"Mr. Richard, I assume you handle your daughter's bookings?"

Papa smiled at Seamus, patting him on the back. "For the moment, yes."

"You've seen Jacob Amos laying limestone," Waldmann gestured in the direction of his building, "just a piece to the west of here, yes?"

Seamus and Papa shared a chuckle. "Why, now that you mention it, indeed I have!"

"I will double whatever Millie's rate is in October if she will do me the honor of being the house violinist when that stone building is finished."

Puffing his cigar, Papa didn't hesitate. "Triple."

"Done," Waldmann nodded, smacking the table with his whisky glass. He stood up to shake hands all around with such German vigor Papa's arm nearly came off.

"This is some wood seller you work for," Papa said to Seamus.

"Glad I could be of help, Mr. Waldmann," Seamus announced.

"I will see you in October, gentlemen." Waldmann turned toward Millie to bow deeply, like he'd just had a vision of the Madonna with Child, their eyes meeting as Millie sent Vivaldi into the Minnesota sky. Waldmann shook his head in disbelief as he turned to leave, finding Shearn at the door, red with Irish rage.

"You bloody kraut," Shearn spit out.

"Vivaldi is wasted on your...ahem...'patrons'", Waldmann replied, walking out past him, westward toward his stone building. Papa and Seamus began a standing ovation for Millie as she finished, beaming. They told her the news.

"What shall I wear??" Millie shouted with excitement.

"Why not purple?" Seamus suggested. "The color of royalty!"

The cure for the panic

The town of Nininger, Minnesota, 25 miles south of St. Paul on the Mississippi River, came as fast as it went, like a mushroom. Governor Alexander Ramsey's brother in law, John Nininger, platted a town named after himself in 1856, began selling lots that October, and by the next October, 1857, it was doomed to vanish. Unlike Anton Waldmann's timing, which never seemed to fail, John Nininger's timing could not have been worse.

Pioneer fever took such hold of Philadelphia's John Nininger that upon arrival in Minnesota, he envisioned the town named after himself to one day dwarf all others, a port that would beat St. Paul to the river traffic by those 25 miles southward. It would be the "Backbone City" of the west. Bigness was so assumed that a hotel Nininger conjured for friends to invest in for his town would be named "Mammoth Hotel". He laid out 3,800 plats, on a map of near virgin land, with the ease of a child creating a very big tic tack toe grid with a crayon. All that remained was the selling.

Nothing in all the annals of human history was ever sold with more vigor than Nininger, by Mr. Nininger. He enlisted numerous Philadelphia associates to spread the Good News of, but first invest in, this imminent frontier metropolis named after their fellow investor. The most prolific such Philadelphian was 25-year-old attorney Ignatius Donnelly, soon to be christened the "Sage of Nininger" by everyone in St. Paul. The Great Seer Donnelly would go on to be the last person living on the land once known as Nininger; after all, he did own it. A future congressman, philosopher, concocter of what today we know as "fake news", etc. upon etc., Donnelly earned another nickname in his old age, "Apostle of Protest". Donnelly's most devoted protestation, pondered well into old age, was that in fact, it was Lord Byron who authored Shakespeare's plays, not the bard himself, in a heavily researched volume Donnelly entitled *The Great Cryptogram*. Donnelly's first publication, foreshadowing such coming wisdom, was *The Emigrant Aid Journal*, Nininger's first, and only, "newspaper", which Donnelly circulated mostly in Philadelphia, New York, riverboats from New Orleans, on Atlantic steamers, to sell lots to immigrants. Its first issue proclaimed on the front page, "Dost thou know how to play the fiddle? 'No', answered Themistocles, 'But I understand the art of raising a little village into a great city.'" Within months of John Nininger conjuring it to existence in October, 1856, Donnelly's art of Themistocles painted such a masterpiece that by the following spring, it required a fortune to buy a Nininger plot off his tic tack toe grid.

At its height in summer, 1857, Nininger claimed a thousand inhabitants, most of whom were investors not yet actually there, and never would be. At most, a few hundred people built homes; no more than 300 ever voted for anything in Nininger. Donnelly managed to elect himself mayor by a vote of 113-3 in February, 1858. Donnelly's home, of course, was the grandest building, complete with an "observatory" on the roof. A boomtown did emerge that boom summer of 1857, with sawmills, town halls, the first trappings an assumed flood of migrants would require once they inevitably placed Nininger in its rightful place in the pantheon beside Rome, Paris, Sparta, the like. Alas, the kingdom come never came.

No one in St. Paul had ever heard of the Ohio Life Insurance and Trust Co., until the newspapers were filled with it after August 24, 1857, the day it went belly up under the weight of fraud and bad investments, setting off an immediate, spiraling collapse of every railroad scheme, land scheme, this or that scheme everywhere. The ensuing Panic of 1857 exposed that the boom years had inflated a casino the size of America, above which Nininger floated as just one of countless tiny fizzy bubbles. Every rugged individualist American with a dream and/or prayer got in before it was too late, which in actual fact was, too late. John Nininger sank smack into the middle of the panic, his map of phantom plots now swarmed by a whirlwind of debts and fleeing investors. His "sage" Donnelly rushed to the ramparts with ever more pamphlets and papers to proclaim, "Cure for the Panic. Emigrate to Minnesota! Where no banks exist." In the 1860 census, 469 people lived in Nininger. By 1865,

Donnelly was on the federal payroll as a Republican congressman, the town nearly emptied, and Nininger himself moved to Alabama to get into the cotton business, proving his timing yet again precisely the opposite of Anton Waldmann's.

Waldmann was glued to the newspapers, ear to the ground, his network as a wood seller to riverboats activated in all directions, to listen for any snippet of information he could gather that crash September of 1857. All the news was bad. St. Paul's papers, a blizzard of pioneer boosterism since the first one came off the press in 1849, couldn't hide the string of Minnesota's biggest banks closing week after week, land prices plummeting, people fleeing. So little hard currency existed in St. Paul, county governments were forced to mint their very own "scrip" to replace the bank notes suddenly gone. Anton's wife Mina worried terribly. She started moving the couple into the upstairs of the stone building on Forbes Street before Jacob Amos laid the last stone outside. She felt its three-foot thick stone walls were rather timely just then.

Being stubborn Germans, Anton and Mina planned to open the saloon that October, and come hell, high water, or financial panic, open it would. Anton had planned well ahead, two record years for steamboats having filled their coffers. Jacob Amos was already paid for his stonework. Steamboat traffic would fall to nearly nothing, of course, but Anton already expected that anyhow, as soon as the first railroad came in. St. Paul's population would decrease, with many fleeing town to find land to farm to survive. But Anton was confident one demand could never be satiated, for lager bier, and a warm place to drink it. So, bit by bit, Mina made the stone building a home, turning Anton and Amos into taste testers for the saloon's menu.

"I can taste no more, Mina," Anton complained, dropping a fork onto his plate from the tenth or so bratwurst he'd tried that day. "They are all...how do we say it English?...delicious." Mina insisted on English in the home. Amos helped himself to Mina's homemade spaetzle. His final days of stonework looming, Amos thrilled in the menu testing, knowing it wouldn't last.

"You work too hard, Anton, just eat," Mina instructed her husband, putting some kraut onto his plate. "Have the wurst with the mustard, I made it special." Anton relented, did as told, and once the mustard did its work, he put down his newspaper in awe.

"This mustard must be on the menu," Anton delighted. "Jacob, take some home with you." Mina didn't like to worry aloud about the state of things, but every so often, she'd remind Anton of the world their saloon was opening into. Giving away mustard would have to be carefully done, if at all.

"We will have to adjust the menu prices," Mina hinted with a smile. Anton looked at his wife with love.

"Downward," Anton declared, smiling at Amos. "Most of this food will come free with a lager, don't you agree Mina?" Mina grinned at her husband's optimism. They would never argue over money, least of all in front of a guest.

"The wursts will never be free," she laughed, "unless you would like to grind the meat and stuff the linings yourself, my love!"

"Are you still planning to hire that fiddler girl?" Amos asked.

"We have a deal, I will honor it, " Anton insisted.

"A German bier saloon must have music," Mina agreed. Anton suddenly remembered his fiddler was betrothed to Seamus Dooley, one of his woodstackers, who most certainly just lost his fortune, what there was of it. Anton paused, remembering how proud Seamus was to grow from a lowly Irish woodstacker boy at the Upper Landing into a young St. Paul businessman, master of his world. Anton sighed.

Mina watched her husband's thoughts course across his face, from worry to sadness for the young fiddler couple's precarious future. The deep realization sank in that he was opening a business at the beginning of a national depression. His saloon would be competing with dozens offering far more immediate, consequence-free escape from their escalating troubles, harder liquor, quicker drowning of their sorrows. As he turned to Mina, he saw in her eyes his same determination that their saloon, come what may, had to be the best saloon in St. Paul for the duration of the coming calamitous years. The boom days were over, the hard ones just begun. St. Paul would need his new business, its beer, and its music.

Mina asked, "Did you not say this fiddler is the finest in St. Paul?" Striking his fork into the plate of Mina's homemade German delicacies, Anton Waldmann charged ahead.

"Yes, and she will need this saloon." Down went another bratwurst.

9 UNIONTOWN, MD

June 30, 1863

Private Rasselas Mowry of Company A enjoyed his first quiet summer morning in nearly a month with a cup of coffee. He strolled through the First Minnesota's camp as the sun rose, lighting up the rolling hills of Pennsylvania to the north, birds chirping. The promise of a day's rest in Uniontown kept practically the entire regiment asleep on the ground, so the bustle outside the officers' tents stood out, where the officers' body servant in striped pants busily prepared breakfast.

"G'mornin', sir!" Toby called to Mowry, happy to see someone else awake.

"What are you doing up so early?" Mowry asked,

approaching with his coffee.

"I's 'bout to ask you the same! Well," Toby replied as he gathered mess kits around the regimental staff campfire, "officers a-sleepin' in. Gettin' breakfast ready for 'em. Had 'em quite a night! Ladies of this town threw 'em a big dance!"

"A dance??"

"Fightin' up north sho is different," Toby chuckled, shaking his head.

"Just for officers..."

Toby grinned. "Juuuuust for officers! Lotta things just for officers, like me!"

"Did you loan Colonel Adams your striped pants for the occasion?" Mowry joked. Toby just smiled. "How come you're so fond of stripes anyway, Toby?"

"Oh, sir," Toby sighed, "Just like 'em I s'pose. Had to take 'em off in that dust up, couple days ago, down the road a piece, dem rebs saw 'em so was a-shootin' at me!"

"So we all heard," Mowry laughed.

"Got to clean 'em, though. More coffee for you sir?"

Mowry joked, "I really shouldn't be drinking

officers' coffee, now, should I, Toby."

"Oh, they'll be sleepin' a good long while," Toby laughed, "rolled into camp pretty late, and well entertained! I'll get more goin', just now gettin' hot, here ya go, secret's safe with me!" Toby filled Mowry's tin cup. "You should get more rest today, sir, seems gonna be some fightin' 'round here."

Raising his cup to Toby as he walked on, Mowry returned to Company A via its "German neighborhood", spread out in the regiment's hasty encampment just north of the little village of Uniontown, Maryland, near Big Pipe Creek in the Appalachian foothills. The Germans of Company A stuck together, speaking German, reading the German newspapers, singing German marching songs, wishing they'd had beer, which was forbidden. Mowry, the Rhode Island Yankee of the company, was an honorary member of the German platoon, through his friendship with Corporal Peter Marks in St. Paul before enlistment back home.

Marks sat in the morning sunshine on the grassy ground, alternating between staring at three envelopes of mail he hadn't yet opened, and his aching feet. "You ever gonna read those?" Mowry asked sarcastically.

"Maybe," Marks replied. "Looks like we get a rest here. These feet are a mess." Another hot summer day had dawned, three weeks of them having burned the faces of the First Minnesota to red and their feet to blisters, marching constantly to chase Lee's Army of Northern Virginia, headed north. Private Charles Mueller rolled over on the ground nearby, yawning himself awake.

"Thirty three miles yesterday by my count," Mueller said rubbing his eyes, "makes this ground the finest bed I've ever slept in."

"Where's the captain?" Marks asked Mowry.

"Toby tells me the ladies of the town threw a ball last night for the officers," Mowry replied. "Coates is probably still in his tent."

"A ball??" Mueller asked, amazed anyone in the Army of the Potomac had the energy to attend a ball, let alone clean uniforms for it.

"Imagine that," Mowry smiled, "a place called Uniontown, throwing a ball for the Union army."

Marks reached for his haversack. "This town loves us! I've got a bag full of biscuits from our parade through town last night!" Looking in his bag, Marks found more than biscuits. "And apple butter...and ham!"

"Half the regiment is gonna be in town today collecting breakfast from the ladies," Mowry speculated.

"They'll get enough for dinner, too," Marks chuckled.

"Fightin' up north sure is different," said Mueller,

rolling back over to sleep more in his dusty uniform. While Mowry stood sipping his coffee, Marks dug into his biscuits and apple butter, tended to his feet, leaving the envelopes lying in the grass next to him, ignored. Mowry had never seen a soldier so disinterested in mail as Marks. Normally, if a soldier was lucky enough to receive mail, it was devoured on the spot of its delivery. For Corporal Peter Marks, mail was just another item to carry in the bag on his back. Sometimes he read it, sometimes he left it behind in the campfire. If Marks did read his mail, Mowry knew to avoid him that day. Because Marks kept these three letters with him since their march began three weeks ago, Mowry figured he'd read those, at which point The Depressed Peter Marks would soon arrive. No one liked that fellow, who was no good to anyone in a fight. Better that Peter's mail is unread, Mowry thought. A battle's coming, everyone could feel it.

Standing over the envelopes with his coffee, Mowry could tell one of Peter's letters was from St. Paul, so he became nostalgic, pulling a well worn, faded blue handkerchief from his pocket to wipe away the early sweat of the First Minnesota's last restful day before a whirlwind took them into history.

10 MAPS

GHOSTS OF PLUM RUN

MAG & FISHER'S CEMETERY RIDGE

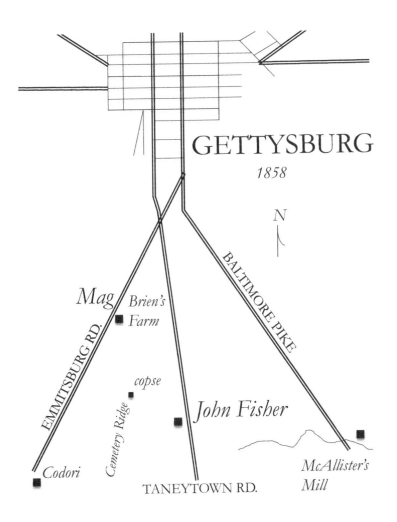

GETTYSBURG

1858

N

Mag

EMMITSBURG RD.

Brien's Farm

BALTIMORE PIKE

copse

Cemetery Ridge

John Fisher

Codori

TANEYTOWN RD.

McAllister's Mill

GHOSTS OF PLUM RUN

PETER MARKS' ENGLAND

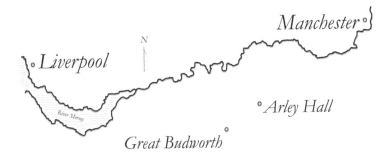

RASELLAS MOWRY'S SMITHFIELD

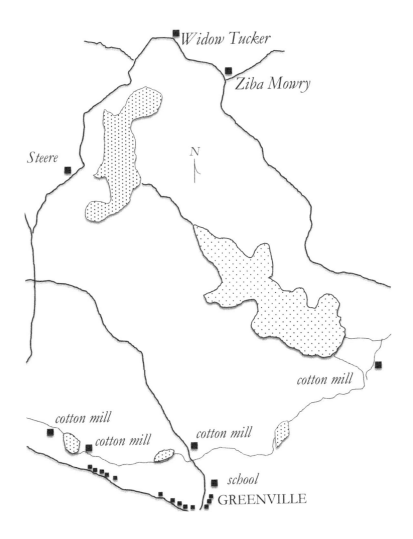

Widow Tucker

Ziba Mowry

N

Steere

cotton mill

cotton mill

cotton mill

cotton mill

cotton mill

school

GREENVILLE

GHOSTS OF PLUM RUN

MILLIE'S ST. PAUL

Papa's farm,
5 miles

N

Henry Shearn's
saloon

Mississippi River
Upper Landing,
350 yards

Anton Waldmann's
saloon

GHOSTS OF PLUM RUN

ABOUT THE AUTHOR

A lifelong Clevelander, Tim Russo was born in Slavic Village to Don J. Russo and Mary Ann Krakowski. As far as can be known, all Tim's great grandparents were immigrants, Polish and Bohemian on Mom's side, all Italian (Sicilian especially) on Dad's. Tim spent his 4 first years of life in the house behind Grandma Krakowski's at 6610 Hosmer Ave. in Cleveland, the next 7 in Old Brooklyn across the Cuyahoga River from Grandma's, and since then has lived in Middleburg Hts., a graduate of Berea High School ('85), Cleveland State Univerisity ('89, '17), and Case Western Reserve School of Law ('94). In between, Tim traveled the world working in politics and international relations, always returning home.

timrusso.org

Made in USA - Kendallville, IN
1172827_9798643622239
09.30.2020 0837